MY TRAVEL COMPANION

ROM COM NOVEL

KEERTHANA SARIN

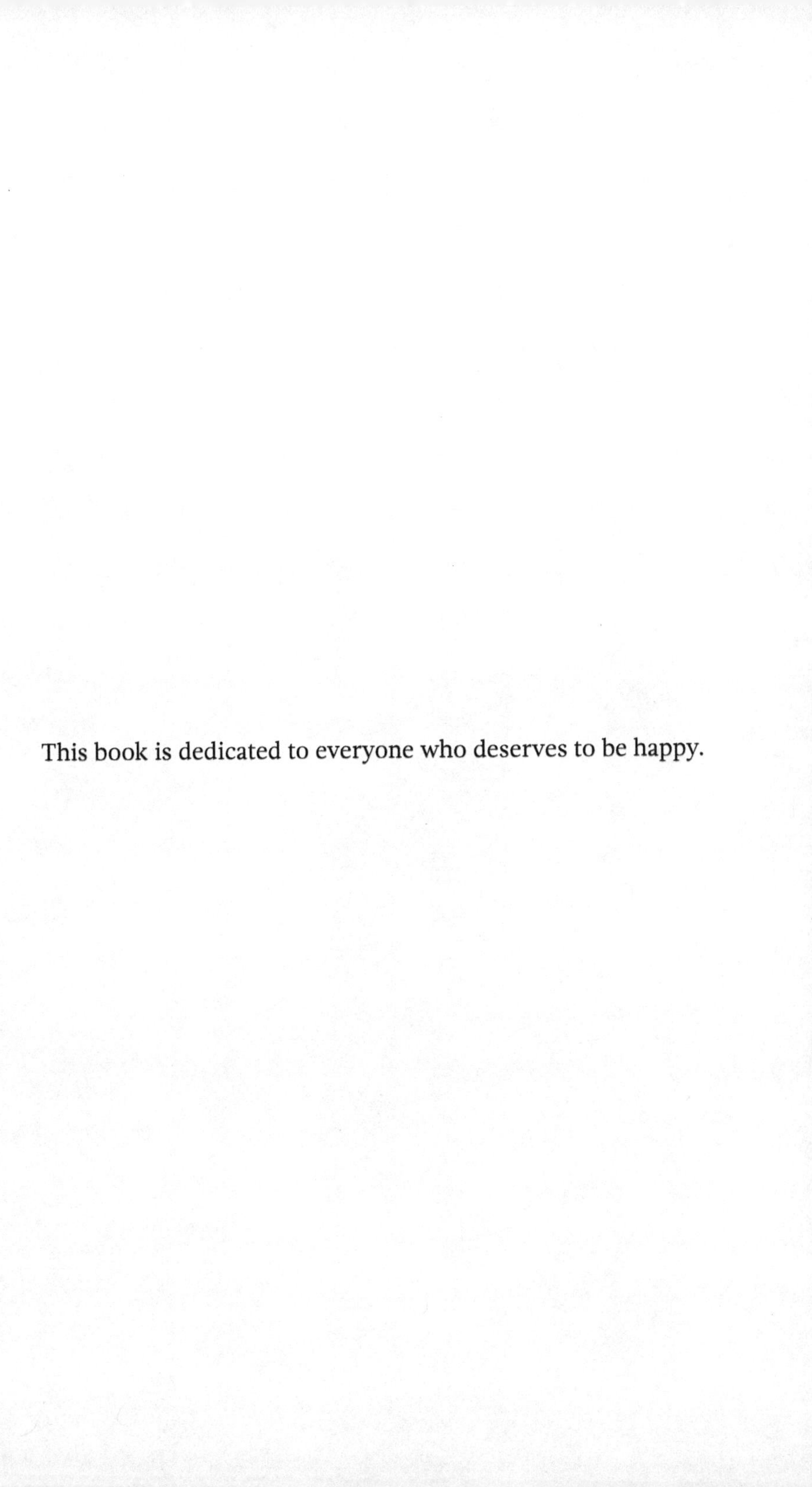

This book is dedicated to everyone who deserves to be happy.

Contents

Foreword   *vii*

Acknowledgements   *ix*

Prologue   *xi*

1. THE JOURNEY BEGINS   1

2. ALEXITHYMIA   4

3. MUNNAR   6

4. LOST   9

5. THE THORN BUSH   12

6. ATONEMENT   16

7. ANAMUDI PEAK   18

8. ON THE BUS   20

9. IN THE BANGALORE PALACE   25

10. LITTLE HAPPINESS   28

11. THE PARADISE   32

12. THE CONFESSION   37

13. AN EMOTIONAL ROLLERCOASTER   42

14. A FUTURISTIC QUESTION   46

15. MYSORE   49

16. THE VOYAGE   52

17. TALKING   56

18. A SWEET FAREWELL   64

19. IN THE TRAIN   68

20. MUMBAI   73

21. DO YOU LIKE FLYING   84

22. REALISATION   91

23. SKY DIVING   98

Contents

24. MUMBAI TO TRIVANDRUM   107

25. BACK TO REGULAR LIVES   117

26. LOVE AND HURT   122

27. THE UNLUCKY ROSE   126

28. REALITY HITS   130

29. WHEN DOCTOR BECAME MEDIATOR   132

30. EUPHORIA   140

EPILOGUE   143

ABOUT THE AUTHOR   149

Foreword

My Travel Companion' is a light-hearted novel that examines life from a variety of perspectives.

Everybody is a traveller by birth. While we encounter new people and go through a range of emotions on our journeys, we will all eventually arrive at our destination—death.

The story begins with Sheetal, an analogy for those who, for an array of reasons, neglect to live their lives. Bitter experiences are inevitable on life's journey. Sometimes, these painful events may hinder our ability to live the joyful existence we deserve.

Even though Kiran had harsh and difficult experiences, he never gave up on trying to find joy in the little things. Unlike those who concealed their genuine selves out of fear of being judged, he is not frightened of being himself.

As the book's author, I can promise you that this piece of art will make you feel happy and relieved from the stress of your hectic lives.

Thank you for joining this journey.
With warm regards,
Keerthana Sarin.

Acknowledgements

I would like to acknowledge my friends and family for helping and encouraging me with this book.

My sincere gratitude to travel vloggers for their visits, experiences, and knowledge sharing about many locations. The majority of the locations covered in this book are ones I haven't been to.

I express my gratitude to all of the readers of "Who is the serial killer?", my first book.

Prologue

"May I come in, sir?"

"Yes". She entered and gave a letter to the Manager.

The manager asked, "What's the matter?"

Sheetal replied, "Sir, I require 2 weeks leave." The Manager's eyes widened and asked "Any emergency?"

She replied, "No, I want to go on a trip. Sir, I hope you will consider my request."

The middle-aged manager took his specs and read the letter. He was confused about this. It was quite usual for him to read leave request letters but Sheetal was exceptional. She rarely took any leave.

The manager said, "Your leave is sanctioned. Are you going with your family or friends?" Sheethal said, "I am going alone".

The manager said, "OK, wish you a happy journey".

Sheetal said "Thank you" in a cold voice and went.

Sheetal was busy with her work and she thought, "I will come here again after 2 weeks or maybe it's my last day."

During the lunch break, every employee sat together no one was left alone except Sheetal. They discussed her unusual leave.

One of the employees named Ganga said "I was shocked when Sachin sir informed me about her leave and handed over her work to me. Even our Manager Sachin sir didn't have this much of attendance, like Sheetal".

Sajan replied, "You are right sis, I even thought she is a robot. She always came early and if she had pending work, she would stay here. And I never saw her smiling. Every time her face is the same, emotionless face.

Yamuna replied, "That's correct, she has no emotions. Once I felt sympathy towards her because she was always lonely and I tried to talk with her and become friends. She behaved rudely towards me."

Yadav commented, "Anyway, we should appreciate her parents for naming her "Sheetal". Cold- hearted woman". Everybody laughed.

Sheetal ate her lunch and went to wash her hands. And sat in the chair of the cashier and continued her work.

The time reached 5 PM; she arranged the files carefully, and she exited the bank. She glanced at the bank for a second, drove her bike and went.

CHAPTER I

THE JOURNEY BEGINS

Sheetal parked her bike in the parking area of Angelina's beauty salon. She entered and sat on the vacant chair. A staff came and asked, "Mam do you want hair colour?" Sheetal asked, "Where is Angelina?"

The staff continued, "Mam she is busy, I will help you?" Sheetal raised her voice and said, "WHERE IS ANGELINA? I DON'T WANT YOUR SERVICE".

Her shouting shocked the staff and customers. Angelina rushed and said, "Sorry madam, I am here." Angelina began to chop off her hair. People were confused because Sheetal, who had short hair, still cutting her hair.

After 5 minutes, Angelina completed her work and Sheetal paid the money and went. The staff asked, "What kind of lady is that? How rude? I just asked politely if she wanted hair colour for this silly reason. She just behaved so rudely."

Angelina replied, "Well, she has been my customer from the beginning of this salon. Can you believe she had long and thick hair once like actress Kavya Madhavan?"

The staff expressed shock and asked, "What?" I can't believe it." Angelina continued, "She came for the first for a haircut. She had long and thick hair and asked me to cut it all. I was shocked and then she said she wanted to donate her hair. I will never forget that day. Her courage amazed me to cut her long hair. From that day onwards, she continues the same hairstyle. Almost more than 10 years."

The staff commented, "Your customers are interesting."

Angelina replied, "She is a regular customer. I think she came here every 2 months for a haircut. She doesn't like anyone except me cutting her hair because I know her appropriate needs. You are a newcomer, that's why you don't know about it. Anyway, handling a variety of customers is one of the features of this job."

Sheetal returned to her home. Her parents were with her. But Sheetal was not close to her parents that much. She gave money, bought medicines and helped them when they required her help. Apart from that, there was no emotional bonding. After coming from the office, she just went to her room and cooked her food. She always isolated herself from others.

She packed her bag; she didn't carry a lot of stuff for this journey because it was kinda like an adventure journey. She just informed her parents that she will not be at home for 2 weeks and went.

Departing from Trivandrum, she boarded a train to Ernakulum. She took the window seat and lost herself in her thoughts. She saw one girl pampering her little sister, which took her to the memories of her late elder sister.

Her elder sister, Thennal, was Sheetal's happiness. Thennal was 4 years old when Sheetal came to this world. Normally, older kids will have a little hate towards their sibling at the initial stage because they might feel all attention will go to the new kid.

Thennal was overjoyed to see Sheetal, in contrast to the other children. Sheetal was valued as a treasure by Thennal. She was the ideal sibling. For Sheetal, Thennal was willing to give up even her happiness.

Thennal once took Sheetal's hair care because of her care. Sheetal's hair was thick and long. In the arts, athletics, and academia, Thennal supported her. She wished for the happiness and well-being of her younger sister.

Their bond didn't endure too long.

When Thennal was studying in college, she fainted and was taken to the hospital. Later, they discovered she had a very rare disease. She was near death. The doctor suggested an operation, which has a 50-50 chance. But it was costly.

Their parents wanted Thennal to live a little more, so they took all their savings and assets for her treatment and medicines. Sheetal was deeply depressed. She couldn't imagine a life without her sister.

She prayed to every god she knew.

The operation was successful. Thennal regained consciousness. After earning her degree, she looked for work, but it was just for a year. Unfortunately, she faced severe health issues and died. Her sudden passing was unforeseen. She displayed not even the slightest hint of illness.

After hearing this heartbreaking news, she didn't cry. She sat on the chair and her face became emotionless. 1000s of thoughts ran through her mind. She didn't cry when she saw the body; she hid all her emotions. That day she lost her soul, joy, hope, faith and even a smile.

Everything around her felt alien to her. She desired the presence of her sister. From that day onwards, her fate towards God had faded.

Her thick, long hair was chopped off. She wanted to cut herself off from her bliss and become someone else entirely.

She couldn't remain idle; her family was going on a debt trap. Her family couldn't sustain the salary of her parents. She was in the last year of her degree.

Then she cracked a bank test and got a job as a cashier at a bank. In her mind, there were only three words:- WORK, EARN, and PAY. She isolated herself from every human being and completely concentrated on her job.

A few years later, she was able to pay off her debt and break free from the vicious circle of debt. She then began setting money aside for her parents. And she accomplished it. She consistently set aside money for herself as well.

She was in her early 30s now, and she had no optimism for the future. She had zero desire to stay alive in this world. She has lived up to this point to provide for both her parents and to pay back the loans, which she has done.

She sensed nothingness. She decided to travel alone, and she planned to take her own life if provided an opportunity.

CHAPTER II

ALEXITHYMIA

Sheetal breathed the busy air of Kochi. It was a working day, everyone was in a hurry.

Children were in a rush to reach their school. Youngsters were walking with their friends. And people were going to their respective jobs.

Sheetal was the only person who wasn't hurry. She decided to visit Wonderla, an amusement park. She took the ticket and saw many people there.

No one was alone like her; few came with friends and others with families.

She joined into a ride named 360. It was one of the famous rides and people usually got afraid just by seeing it because it rotated the heads and bodies of people and made them unconscious sometimes.

Sheetal thought she might scream and express her emotions like others. In contrast, while others were laughing, crying, and screaming, Sheetal maintained a state of silence. She wasn't afraid. Maybe she forgot the way of expressing her emotions.

Sheetal had encountered the majority of the rides and games available, yet it had no impact on her. She felt like she didn't deserve to be happy. She never felt she was in depression and never thought about committing suicide.

These years, she had a mission to earn money to pay off debt and help her parents. Their pension fund and fixed deposit were enough for them. She felt like her obligations were over and she had no intention of leaving.

She was neither sad nor happy, just blank.

She walked through Marine Drive and saw a few couples. She was 30 years old, but she never had a lover. Within this era, students attending school may possess diverse experiences, such as former relationships. She never experienced a romantic relationship.

Nobody approached her because she might attack them with her words, and she never thought about approaching anyone.

Sheetal opted to undertake a journey to the well-known tourist destination, Munnar.

CHAPTER III

MUNNAR

She went to the bus station and checked whether there was any bus going to Munnar and she found out that there was a bus but she needed to wait for 30 minutes.

She sat on a bench and scrolled her phone. On the next bench, there was a couple and a young girl. The young girl glanced at Sheetal. And she commented to her parents, "I will cut my hair short like that sister".

Sheetal heard it, and she didn't like the comment of the girl. In reality, the girl liked her hairstyle, but Sheetal got irritated.

There were no vacant seats, so Sheetal wanted to stand for 30 minutes.

Finally, the bus arrived. She already booked the ticket online. She went to a window seat, and she slept.

In her dream,

In a gloomy forest, she got lost. Not even a flicker of light existed.

It seemed like the clouds were about to weep.

She travelled through the woods on foot.

Moreover, she encountered terrifying voices. Racing, she spotted a tunnel.

She dashed inside the tunnel. She got teary and sad, and it continued for ages.

The tunnel appeared to go on endlessly. It had become all dark in the background.

Finally, she saw the light at the end of the tunnel.

She pondered about the strange dream when she woke up. She wasn't certain what it meant and was just puzzled by it.

Munnar was reached via a bus.

The guests were welcomed by the delightful scent of tea leaves. Sheetal was attracted to Munnar because of its placid and cold temperature. A special bond occurred between her and Munnar.

She thought "Munnar is just like me frozen enigmatic, and alone." The perfect location for an ideal farewell.

She decided to go exploring in the village of Vattavada. She became interested in the jungle campaigning activity as she checked out other activities related to this area online.

Sheetal reached the spot. There were many people.

This activity offered tourists to visit the jungle with a guide.

The tour guide guided Sheetal, a science teacher, and her fellow students. These students were 7th and 8th students who visited this forest on a study tour. They aimed to know more about various plants.

The female teacher who was in her late 40s couldn't digest the fact that a girl who had short hair and showed courage to travel alone. The teacher decided to poke her nose at Sheetal by asking unnecessary questions.

The teacher asked, "Hey girl, do you think it is safe to travel alone? Aren't you aware of the events happening in this world"?

Sheetal replied, "How do you know I am travelling alone? Are you a schoolteacher or detective?"

The teacher laughed and said, "Never mind, also don't wear T-shirts and jeans while travelling alone and girls must want long hair. Look at my hair."

Sheetal lost her patience. "You should concentrate on your job. Take care of your kids, not me." The teacher murmured, "An arrogant and spoiled girl can't even know how to respect elders."

The teacher was careless about the students, poor students were taking notes and if they asked questions, she might shout. She hated field trips.

Suddenly there was a flash of lightning and thunder that made a terrible noise. The students took off dashing in different directions. The teacher and tour guide couldn't handle all of those children by themselves.

Also, Sheetal sought to aid her. Sheetal noticed one boy run in a different direction.

Sheetal approached and caught him. The boy followed the right direction that she instructed.

The wind blew hard, and Sheetal's eyes were filled with a small bit of dirt. She cleaned he face and massaged her eyes.

The weather soon returned to normal. She looked and saw that everyone had gone. She recalled the tour guide's statement that "everyone should be in the group." It must be hard to figure out if someone gets lost, and the jungle must be unsafe after six in the evening.

Sheetal tightened up briefly. She was staring at her phone. There wasn't a range. Although she was ready to die, she wasn't ready to die here.

The attacks on wild creatures disturbed her. She spent nearly twenty minutes wandering through the jungle. Everything resembled alike, such as the trees, sky, and plants. She attempted to imagine what would happen if the wild creatures arrived and attacked her.

Unexpectedly, she discovered the massive bush's leaves moving. She seemed as rigid as stone. And from there as well she heard a voice designed to scare her. She chose to turn and flee. The voice was no longer threatening, and the bushes had stopped moving when she turned around.

Suddenly, someone said, "HELLO," in front of Sheetal. He was a charming, glasses-wearing man in his early thirties. He was a tourist as well.

Sheetal was angry but she maintained calm. She merely walked forward.

He remarked, "Hey stop, are you sure that direction is correct?" as he followed her.

Turning, Sheetal inquired, "Are you familiar with this direction?"

With a smile, he responded, "No, I lost myself, just like you did. Together, let's find the right way.

She didn't like his presence. But it was not safe to figure out the way alone. She nodded.

CHAPTER IV

LOST

"Note the texture of the leaves," he continued. "People walked on this path, and the leaves looked trampled," he said, gesturing in the proper direction.

Sheetal followed behind him.

"Well, my name is Kiran, and I work as an advocate," he said.
   Sheetal stayed silent.

"Hey, what's your name?" Kiran asked.

Without enthusiasm, Sheetal rolled her eyes and responded, "I am Sheetal, working at a private bank." She disliked having talks.
   Kiran answered, "Well, I see. I don't particularly appreciate travelling alone; I'm not very good at it. I had even made trip plans with a travel companion. We decided to go travelling. Sadly, his mother fell sick, so he was unable to accompany me. Since you are travelling alone, Sheetal, would you be my travel companion if that's okay?
   Sheetal was already irritated by his conversation. All she wanted was to get away from his words and the woods. She remained silent.
   Kiran smiled and said, "Don't worry about it; we are going through the same path. Yes, we almost reached the entrance."
   The tour guide looked tense and he was about to search for them. Seeing them, he approached and said, "Thank God, I was tensed this madam got in danger. Luckily, you were there."
   Kiran gestured to the tour guide to stop telling him he wasn't new in the jungle.

Sheetal gave him a furious expression after being startled. Kiran gave an uneasy smile.

"PERVERT, so you already know the path and you just pretend you had lost to flirt with me?" exclaimed Sheetal angrily. Her remark was noticed by many individuals.

Kiran answered, "Hear me out as well. Yes, this is not my first visit to this place. This is my second experience. But in the process of capturing a few photos, I got lost. Furthermore, I am a person who frequently gets lost. I couldn't figure out which was the right path. I was relieved to find you since I felt like I had someone to help me to choose the right route."

Sheetal realised he was correct.

"Don't say something unclear," Kiran murmured, fixing her gaze on the tour guide. "Try to finish it, or else misunderstandings may arise".

The tour guide grinned and nodded before heading out.

"Sorry," Sheetal whispered, feeling bad for him.

Kiran responded, 'Sorry' you just slandered me in front of these people. Everybody looked at me and they might have thought that I was a pervert. What would happen if anyone came and beat me or arrested me for harassment?"

With an odd expression, Sheetal said, "Hey, don't overthink this. I apologized" and said, "Enough."

"I want compensation," Kiran murmured, staring at her.

Sheetal inquired, "What kind of payment?" She couldn't figure it out.

"I want compensation since you commit something that threatens my dignity," Kiran stated. Buy a meal for me.

In some way, Sheetal agreed.

CHAPTER V

THE THORN BUSH

They went to a nearby restaurant and placed their tea and food orders.

"The cold climate in Munnar is so peaceful, right?" inquired Kiran.

Sheetal sipped the tea, nodding.

Meals were supplied by the supplier.

Kiran remarked, "Delicious food. At times, all I can think about is purchasing some tea plantation land and moving here to live like a landlord."

Sheetal gave a nod.

"Can I ask you a question?" inquired Kiran.
    "Yes," Sheetal replied.

"Will you be my travel companion?"

In response, Sheetal said, "I don't want anybody's company," right away.

"Alright, after this meal, we can separate," Kiran answered.

Sheetal said, "Alright."
    Kiran continued, "Well, I have a request; I have a habit of collecting memories. If you don't mind, can we take a picture?"

"Whatever," Sheetal answered.

As they consumed their food, they noticed a park across from the restaurant.

Kiran remarked, "Look, that place is a perfect location to take snapshots".

Sheetal nodded, with a bit of guilt towards Kiran.

Sheetal felt a little pain in her arm, and when she checked it she saw one scratch. Kiran saw it and asked what was wrong.

"Nothing," she murmured. I believe that any thorny bush in the forest caused me to get a scratch.

Kiran asked, "Where just show me?" now.

He was surprised to see that and said, "Well, this is caused by a thorny bush."I forgot its name. It was the same wound that I had. Additionally, I was told by my tour guide that I would shortly pass out. I didn't give it much thought. Fortunately, I had fallen close to the tent. I woke up, I guess, after thirty minutes. You ought to head to your hotel right away.

"Stop making stories, look, I'm okay," Sheetal retorted. "Not even a hint of weakness on my part. Just take the picture and walk away if that's what you want to do."

Kiran was perplexed as well and wondered, "Why didn't she feel dizzy? She might be healthier than I am haha.

With a questioning look on her face, Sheetal said, "What are you waiting for, just take the photo?"

Taking his phone, Kiran turned on the camera. He saw suddenly that Sheetal was faint and on the verge of passing out. Kiran took hold of her.

"Sheetal.. Sheetal, are you ok?" Kiran called. He realised she'd fallen unconscious. He located one bench after searching for empty ones. He placed her on the bench after carrying her. She was dozing when he made her sit on the bench.

Kiran sought any kind of remedy for this over the phone with the tour guide.

"Sir, the affected person should lie down," he remarked. Don't worry, the affected person will awaken after thirty minutes.

Kiran used her bag as a pillow and rested on the bench. He left her there because she didn't enjoy his company.

A football was about to strike him when he decided the decision to walk away. He grabbed the ball out of anger. A child of eight years old approached and requested the ball.

"It's a park, not a playground," Kiran remarked. Get out of here and head to the playground.

Suddenly, a big, muscular man arrived. He appeared to be a WWE fighter and stood approximately 6 feet tall.

"WHO THE HELL ARE YOU TO ORDER MY KIDS TO STOP PLAYING?" he screamed. "Alright, if you defeat me, we'll move from this park to the playground.

"Sir, I'm sorry, you guys enjoy," Kiran whispered his eyes widening. Please accept my apology for my error.

"YOU ARE INTELLIGENT," he yelled back.

Kiran simply wanted to get out of there. The sight of the man alarmed him. He turned to go, but his thoughts hesitated to leave Sheetal when he saw her.

"I know she's so cold and rude, but it's not safe to leave her alone like this," he thought to himself. If a football hits her in the face, what will happen? Or did someone hurt her?

Kiran wanted to sit near her, but she was dozing off. The only thing to do was make Sheetal fall asleep on Kiran's lap. Kiran could make sure that the football wouldn't touch Sheetal because there were no empty benches.

In some way, Kiran rested her head on his lap. By determining whether the football would hit or not, he felt very accomplished. He had such an exhausted look.

They were noticed by an old couple. They went up to Sheetal and Kiran. "What happened to your wife?" inquired the elderly guy. Is she ill?

"No uncle, she works in the IT sector," Kiran lied. She didn't sleep for three consecutive days because she had an assignment to finish. I brought her to the park so she could get some fresh air and relax.

The elderly couple expressed their admiration for them, and the elderly woman whispered "See, you were just like this when we first got married. You don't care for me anymore.
"Open your mouth, dear," the elderly guy kindly instructed as he led her to a candy store, where he purchased a gulab jamun while holding her hands. "We are not young to behave like this; we are both diabetes patients," she replied, appearing shy.
"One candy won't kill us," the elderly man commented with a smile. And remarked, "Expressing love has no age, dear."

As Kiran observed this, he couldn't help but think, "I hope their love lasts forever."

CHAPTER VI

ATONEMENT

Kiran had gone insane, gazing at the elderly couple's love. "Love has no age," he declared.

Sheetal had quickly awakened.

Sheetal suddenly got up from his lap, startled beyond belief.

"WHAT THE HELL, WHY DID YOU MAKE ME SLEEP ON YOUR LAP, PERVERT?" she shouted.

Sheetal slapped his face, without even waiting for Kiran to explain.

When the elderly pair noticed it, they came over and the elderly man asked, "What happened to your wife? How come she slapped you?"

Sheetal fixed Kiran's gaze. "Nothing uncle, I accidentally disturbed her, that's why she is stressed," he said with a forced smile.

"He was attempting to keep you from colliding with the football. Don't bother this poor soul, please. The elderly couple left holding hands.

Sheetal asked, "When I become your wife?" as if she were angry.

"All right, tell me what happened," Sheetal said.

"You had fainted, so I put you on this bench," Kiran remarked. I was ready to walk away from you, but there were a few kids playing football, and they could hurt you. I am a human too. I didn't think it was a good idea to leave you alone. I forced you to lie down on my lap so I could shield you from the football. My tour guide also advised me to lay down you.

Sheetal patiently listened to him. Her face caught her attention. She could see the mark caused by the slap on his cheek.

"I don't know if you believe this or not," Kiran said. I am not a pervert, anyhow. I made a mistake when I spoke with you and requested your company for this journey. Goodbye, and I hope to never see you again.

Sheetal held sympathy towards him. It takes her a long time to feel sympathy for someone. She walked behind him and said, "I apologise, Kiran, for how I behaved." Just keep my side in mind as well. I was totally confused.

"Once I considered your apology, you slapped and kept making the same mistake," Kiran replied. Leave me alone, Madam. Stay away from perverts.

"I swear I won't make the same mistake again," Sheetal stated. I am ready to become your travel companion."

Kiran remarked, eyebrows raised. "Do you intend to murder me?"

Stopping him, Sheetal gave him a straight gaze before stating, "Once more, I am saying I am ready to become your travel companion."

"Now that I know you are genuinely ready," Kiran remarked.

She accepted his handshake when he extended it.

They became travel companions.

CHAPTER VII

ANAMUDI PEAK

"You don't have any plans?" Kiran enquired.

Sheetal said, "Of course."

Kiran mentioned, "I would like to make a suggestion." There is a destination. The Anamudi Peak provides a rejuvenating encounter with the splendour of nature.

Kiran had the intention of embarking on an adventure to Anamudi Peak, yet Sheetal tragically chose to end her life while hiking. She considered the idea that others might interpret it as an inadvertent mishap.

They both initiated their hiking expedition. Due to Sheetal's dedication to physical activity and maintaining a healthy lifestyle, she enjoyed a fit physique, which facilitated her successful hike to the peak. Kiran was amazed.

After arriving at a higher point, they took a break.

Kiran began to photograph the peak of Anamudi. "Well, can you take a picture with me?" inquired Sheetal.

Kiran was startled by her question since he didn't expect it to come from her. Kiran and Sheetal took a selfie together.

When Sheetal smiled, Kiran saw it and remarked, "God, you finally showed your teeth."

Sheetal had the notion, "This will be the last picture I take." I was finally able to live in this strange environment, so I smiled.

Kiran clicked the picture.

"Could you send me the picture?" inquired Sheetal. Would it bother you if I uploaded this photo to Instagram?

She provided her Instagram ID to Sheetal. He forwarded the picture.

Kiran answered, "No problem, feel free to post it."

Kiran shared the photo that Sheetal had uploaded as an Instagram story.

Kiran pondered Sheetal's peculiar attitude before considering the possibility that she was enjoying the trip.

Sheetal noticed that Kiran was occupied with trying to capture the beauty of Anamudi.

She closed her eyes and breathed in the fresh air, feeling the cool breeze tousle her short hair. Her mind was moving more quickly than the breeze.

"Sister, my soul left me when you left this world," she thought to herself. Life was not exciting, good. I stopped communicating with everyone, including our parents. I'm always curious about how they adjusted to living without you. If you were alive and I died, that would be preferable.

She tightly closed her eyes and was about to jump. Kiran interrupted her as she was ready to jump, declaring, "Sheetal, we have to leave." I received a call from the jeep driver informing me that rain is expected. If the rain begins, it will be hazardous.

Sheetal glared at him.

In response, Kiran said, "What are you waiting for? Come on, please." Sheetal thought, "I can never die with this guy."

In the evening, they headed to a cafe. They felt the warmth as they drank hot tea.

Kiran remarked, "In this cold climate, sipping a hot tea gives a special experience, right?"

Sheetal nodded.

Kiran asked, "Hey what's your next plan? How many days do you have?"

Sheetal replied, "Well, I have two weeks. I don't have any plans. You can suggest."

Kiran responded, "I think Bangalore will be a good choice. There are botanical gardens, museums, lakes, amusement parks, food streets, etc. And the Bus is also available, so if you are ready we can go."

Sheetal replied, "OK, we can go."

They went to the bus station and boarded a bus.

CHAPTER VIII

ON THE BUS

They got on the bus. Families made up the majority of the passengers.

Kiran took a seat beside Sheetal, who was seated by the window seat

"I hope you are comfortable to sit with me," Kiran remarked. I have no other options because there are no open seats."

"If I say I'm not comfortable, what will you do?" Sheetal rolled her eyes.

"I will ask any other passenger to swap seats," Kiran remarked. Hey, we're travel companions. How are we supposed to travel together if you don't feel comfortable with me?

Sheetal became irritated. "Whatever, you can sit with me."

By the time the bus left, it was almost 4:45 PM, and Munnar wouldn't be reached until 5:30 AM.

"So, why did you decide to go on a solo trip?" Kiran questioned.

There's nothing extraordinary, Sheetal said. Just one haphazard idea."

In response, Kiran said, "Amazing. Then you will most likely be wealthy. Because you had the money and one day you just chose to take a vacation. I had saved money for nearly three years to consolidate my trip expenses."

With a frown, Sheetal replied, "I'm not rich. After all costs, I used to set aside a certain amount of money, which I used for this trip. That concludes it."

"Okay, I get it," Kiran responded.

Sheetal was sitting in the window seat, staring out the window. She also said nothing.

"Don't you get bored looking at the roads, buildings, trees, etc.? Will you sit in this manner for the next eleven hours?"Kiran enquired.

I prefer to be alone. The sky, the buildings, and the roads are preferable to interacting with people," Sheetal remarked.

Kiran asked back, "Really? Engaging with diverse individuals provides a distinct experience. Human interactions are interesting, in my opinion. I'll learn about new perspectives, experiences, lifestyles, joys, and struggles. Furthermore, personal interaction is a part of my line of work. An advocate must be more socially and communicatively effective."

Sheetal gave a nod.

"I hated the lockdown period so much because I couldn't even leave my house or meet any of my friends at that time," Kiran replied.

In response, Sheetal said, "That was my favourite time." No conversations, no exchanges. I could work from home while sitting at my home."

Kiran appeared shocked. "No comments."

Kiran noticed that Sheetal constantly looked out the window when she spoke. She avoided giving him any glances. He was aware of her dislike of social interaction.

"How will I spend my holidays with her?" he wondered. She's not talking to anyone. We might part ways after our trip to Banglore.

Kiran grabbed his phone and visited Instagram since he was bored. The sight of over ten messages shook him.

"Today is not my birthday, so why is there such a big message today?" he wondered.

He began to go through his direct messages.

After viewing his story, his closest friends responded as follows:

"Who is this? You've finally got a girl".

"Tomboy, you're fond of short hair, right?"

"This is your 2-week journey, right? You kept this a secret from me even though I am your closest buddy, enjoy."

"My brother finally got a girl."

"My brother broke his celibacy hehe."

"When are you getting married?"

Kiran yelled, "Oh my god," as his eyes widened.

Most of the passengers heard him scream.

A young child inquired, "Uncle, what happened?"

Kiran grinned but made no other movements.

"It's probably his girlfriend beat him," muttered an elderly woman.

Kiran and Sheetal both heard that.

Their expressions of irritation were identical, but Kiran's was more intense.

"Why didn't you add a caption to your Instagram story like my travel companion?" Kiran enquired after a few minutes.

In response, Sheetal said, "Is that necessary?"

"Madam, if you don't add any caption and but a picture of a guy, people might think he will be your lover," Kiran flashed, holding back his rage.

Sheetal asked back, "Really?"

Kiran glared at her and replied, "Please read these messages".

Sheetal's eyes followed those words.

She responded, "Just say you are my travel companion or ignore it."

Kiran replied, "Just check your direct messages, then you can understand."

She checked and said, "See, no one replied to my story."

Kiran was taken aback when no one responded to her public account with more than 200 followers. All they saw was her story.

In fact, no one dared to text Sheetal due to her unfriendly nature. She also didn't give their photo much thought as the story's focal point.

People got off the bus about 8 p.m. and headed to a restaurant.

They had chicken curry and chappati ordered.

"Which is your favourite food?" inquired Kiran.

Sheetal spoke "Noodles" without delay.

"Noodles, that's a different answer," said Kiran and smiled.

This is how most children and teenagers respond.

"My sister used to cook chicken noodles when I was a child," Sheetal replied.

Sheetal's expression showed a hint of happiness, Kiran noticed.

"Why did she stop making noodles?" Kiran asked.

In response, Sheetal said, "I finished my meal. Let me wash my hands.

Kiran wondered why she didn't reply to his question, but he got a call from his brother.

Keerthan is the younger brother of Kiran.

Kiran enquired, "Hey, what's wrong? Require funds."

In response, Keerthan said, "My dear bro, you are great." You've finally found a girlfriend. Brother, I will support your love, brother."

"Oh, that's why you called me, my beloved bro," Kiran retorted. She is just my travel companion. And don't think that I will get married and you will be the next.

In a furious reply, Keerthan said, "IDIOT, YOU ARE IN YOUR 30S." HOW WILL I GET MARRIED IF YOU ARE NOT? You will likely pass away alone and force me to pass away too."

"You are barely 27 years old, too young to get married," Kiran remarked.

"TOO YOUNG!" cried Keerthan. MOST OF MY FRIENDS GOT MARRIED AND STARTING HAVING KIDS".

Kiran ended the call.

Sheetal soon arrived.

Hold on for me, Kiran responded. I'll be here shortly.

After ten minutes, the two of them got inside the bus along with every other passenger.

The bus carried on with its trip.

It was nine o'clock now. Sheetal and Kiran were both tired.

Both Kiran and Sheetal yawned.

"I have two head pillows," Kiran remarked, holding out a head pillow to Sheetal. Sadly, my friend was unable to attend, even though he had asked me to bring it. Use this to ensure a good sleep and to avoid generating neck strain."

Sheetal took the pillow for her head.

With a "goodnight," Kiran

Sheetal said good night in response.

They both surrendered to sleep's embrace.

At three in the morning, Sheetal heard a conversation and woke up.

She knew Kiran was speaking in her sleep. "Your honour, I can prove how my client is innocent... My Lord."

"This man can't even stop talking while sleeping," Sheetal thought to herself.

"Habeas Corpus, Rule of Law, Partnership Act," Kiran went on.

Sheetal went to sleep, closing her eyes.

CHAPTER IX

IN THE BANGALORE PALACE

The bus finally arrived in Bangalore.

It was about eight in the morning. Traffic jams caused the bus to arrive late.

"Sheetal, wake up, we arrived in Bangalore," called Kiran when she awakened.

After awakening, Sheetal enquired, "What's the next plan?"

"We have to go to any restaurant and get something to eat," he stated.

Sheetal was also craving food.

They went to a restaurant together and had breakfast.

Sheetal asked, "What's the schedule for today?"

Kiran said, "Bangalore Palace! In addition, do you find museums to be enjoyable? You were a commerce student."

With a small smile, Sheetal answered, "Everything is the same for me."

Kiran was unable to grasp the significance of those six words. By this, she meant that she had no interests at all. Simply following the course of events.

"The museum will only open at 10 AM, so we have two extra hours," Kiran stated. I believe the number of street stores is enormous. Two hours of enjoyment is what's in store.

Sheetal consented.

Sheetal's mental state was somewhat strange. She no longer considered suicide, but she still didn't want to live. She was in a dilemma. She pondered, "I have no idea what will happen. Anyway, follow this garrulous guy through the flow.

Kiran and Sheetal entered the marketing streets, a lot of different varieties of street foods, books, bangles, earrings, dresses, bags, etc.

Sheetal said, "I never thought this much of stores would open at 8 AM."

"You can buy dresses at affordable rates," Kiran remarked.

"I'm going shopping for dresses. Purchase it if you'd like," Kiran added.

Kiran purchased three shirts, Sheetal purchased two T-shirts, two shirts, and one pair of jeans.

"There's a shop if you want awesome kurtas," Kiran added.

In response, Sheetal said, "I don't wear kurtas."

Kiran answered, "Okay."

As they strolled about and took in the beauty of the streets, Kiran noticed a classy shop with stunning earrings.

"If you are interested in earrings, especially jhumakas, you can buy from there," Kiran pointed to it.

Sheetal gave him a two-second gaze.

"Sorry, I forgot you are not a female," Kiran shot back.

Sheetal frowned.

They sampled a variety of street fare.

"It is now 9:10 AM, therefore we may head to the palace, Kiran remarked.

"All right," replied Sheetal.

Upon acquiring the services of an autorickshaw, they arrived at the opulent palace.

"Impressive," Kiran remarked.

After obtaining their ticket from the clerk, they went into the palace.

When Kiran saw something, he announced, "Audio guidance is available." It will be very beneficial.

Sheetal answered, "Yes, we can give it a try."

They proceeded to the counter and picked up a headset and two audio guidance devices.

The majority of the information about the palace was provided via audio guidance, which made its operation spectacular.

After selecting number one on the keypad, Sheetal heard "WELCOME TO BANGALORE PALACE." She thought the audio guidance keypad's layout was good.

In return, Sheetal said, "His presentation was good. I felt like somebody in real life explaining the history."

"The growth of technology is impressive," Kiran remarked.

"Look there, that's the first lift in India," Kiran added.

Sheetal peered at the wood-built lift, its gold workings looking magnificent.

Next, they went to the Darbar library, where they saw several amazing portraits and images depicting different occasions.

The staircase's architectural design was striking.

"Even the royal walls have some stories to tell us," Kiran said, "The beauty of history is her enigmatic nature.

Sheetal gave a nod.

After seeing all the sights inside the palace, they came straight to the path in the garden.

Kiran said, "I appreciate the people who preserve the remains of history."

Sheetal replied, "You are right and now it's afternoon, so we can eat lunch."

Kiran smiled and responded, "I forgot about my hunger because of the excitement lol.

CHAPTER X

LITTLE HAPPINESS

"Whoa, this Mysore Pak tastes so good!" Kiran exclaimed.

Sheetal said, "That's true."

"Well, there's a botanical garden called Lalbagh Park," Kiran retorted. It will undoubtedly provide a revitalising experience.

"All right, we can go," Sheetal answered.

They arrived at Lalbag Park by way of an Uber cab.

It was about 4 p.m. and not very crowded.

There were multiple tiny stores.

Would you like ice cream? Kiran asked. This will be an ideal spot to have ice cream while taking in the scenery."

"We are not kids or teenagers to eat ice cream while walking," Sheetal said. That is such an immature act.

Laughing, Kiran exclaimed, "Immaturity, lol." Would you kindly explain the reasoning behind your icy attitude? Since we are humans, enjoying ice cream and taking in the scenery is not wrong. Why should we give up on our tiny happiness to keep our maturity?

"I know you will never understand," Sheetal shot back. You can buy, eat, and walk if you so choose. You are free to use it. I won't get involved.

Kiran purchased a single chocolate bar and a single bottle of sparkling water.

"This is a water bottle. It must be required of you," told Kiran.

Sheetal took it.

They began to take in the breathtaking beauty of the Lalbagh Botanical Garden as soon as she placed it in her purse.

"Sheetal, Bangalore is known as the city of the garden because own the possession of many beautiful gardens," Kiran remarked.

Sheetal gave a nod.

They came upon numerous gorgeous flowers. The elegance of the blooms stunned them.

Kiran remarked,

"These lovely flowers have a short life, but they never fail to make us happy. They had no concern for how short their lives were."

"Poetry right?" Sheetal asked in reply.

Kiran replied. "Nope, just a fact."

They examined the state of the lake close to the botanical garden.

"What a wonderful lake! I want to swim in it," Kiran exclaimed.

When the young child heard this, she exclaimed, "Uncle, you can't swim there." My parents informed me that it is restricted.

Her parents chuckled.

Kiran got embarrassed.

Kiran received a stern glare from Sheetal, who commented, "Even that child possesses greater knowledge."

Kiran giggled.

They could hear the sound of the water hitting the rough rocks, even though they could only see a small waterfall.

"Even the sound of the waterfalls is calm, but our minds are not," Kiran stated."

Rolling her eyes, Sheetal answered, "Actually, what exactly do you mean?"

"Just think you will understand," Kiran retorted.

To which Sheetal said, "Whatever."

They noticed a gigantic vintage tree. Everyone was taking pictures.

"I'm a little tired," Kiran stated. There are a few empty seats. Could we go sit there, please?"

They went to the emerald-coloured bench and sat.

Sheetal accepted the water and had a sip. "I sweated too much, even though it's not that sunny outside," she remarked.

To which Kiran replied with a smile, "Because you walked a lot."

"Well, I appreciate the cleanliness of this park," Sheetal retorted.

"Exactly," Kiran remarked.

Sheetal decided to snap some photos after grabbing her phone.

"Perfect location for taking pictures? Would you kindly snap a photo of me?" inquired Kiran.

Standing up, Sheetal took a picture of him and presented it to Kiran.

He replied enthusiastically, "Wow, this is going to be my Instagram, WhatsApp profile pics hehe," as his eyes grew big. You are a superb photographer.

Kiran's words triggered an old memory of her. Her sister used to say that one day Sheetal also becomes a talented photographer."

Sheetal sat on the bench, frozen. Kiran noticed her and he understood she was something miserable, so Kiran gave time to her. Kiran was scrolling his phone.

After a while, they walked around the garden, and the peaceful atmosphere made them both feel relaxed.

They were so deeply involved in the botanical garden that they were unaware of how much time had passed.

They abandoned the garden behind.

It was around 5:00 p.m.

"We want to stay at any hotel, right?" Sheetal inquired.

Kiran panicked and exclaimed, "Oh, I forgot about it right now!" Finding a good hotel at a reasonable price is tough. I'm hoping you get it.

In response, Sheetal said, "I was unaware of it. I assumed you would set everything up.

Kiran said, "If I was alone, I could find a cheap lodge and stay there, but with you, I can't."

Sheetal Infuriated., "So you are saying I am the problem?"

Kiran was observing something and ignored Sheetal.

"Hey Kiran, are you even listening to me?" Sheetal asked again.

Kiran ran away leaving Sheetal puzzled. "Kiran—Kiran."

He hurried to prevent a young girl from being hit by a car and saved her. To save a little girl, he picked her up and dashed over to the road.

Her parents came running and gave her a big hug. They were in tears.

Seeing those moments astonished Sheetal; Kiran had shown an unexpected shade of his. She rushed to catch up with him and the family.

"I don't know how to express our gratitude towards you," stated the little girl's father.

There's no need to thank you, Kiran responded with a smile. That's it; that's my moral obligation.

"Brother, you had risked your life for our daughter's life," her mother said, sobbing. We usually can't take our eyes off of her. The bustling market had distracted us for a short while today our attention."

"Don't worry, this little angel's balloon escaped her hands," Kiran reassured. She attempted to grab the balloon. And for that reason, she had entered the road.

Kiran glanced at the little girl and replied in a gentle voice, "Hey don't be careless. Look, your mom is crying." She wiped her mother's tears and said, "Mama, I will never repeat this."Her mother gave her a firm embrace.

"Well, my name is Jacob," her father retorted. This is Grace, my wife. And Olivia is the name given to our daughter. Good to meet you."

Kiran replied, "I am Kiran, and this is Sheetal. We are travel companions."

Grace remarked, "That's why you guys were not familiar? You are from where?"

Kiran replied, "We are from Kerala."

Jacob inquired, "Where are you staying at?"

Kiran replied, "Well. We didn't get an appropriate stay."

Grace answered, "If you guys are comfortable, come to our home. It is not a palace, but it is enough for 5 of us. What's your opinion, Jack?"

"You're right, my dear," Jacob retorted. We extend a warm welcome to Kiran and Sheetal in our home.

Kiran glared at Sheetal.

She gave a nod of affirmation.

CHAPTER XI

THE PARADISE

They got into the couple's vehicle.

Travel Companions were seated in the backseat.

The driver of the vehicle was Jacob. "Well, it looks like we'll be getting home in almost ten minutes," he remarked.

"Well, you guys are from which district?" Grace retorted.

"I am from Kollam," Kiran declared.

Sheetal answered, "I am from Trivandrum."

Grace remarked, "My mother is from Trivandrum. Kerala was a place I used to go on vacations while I was in school. There is a connection between my early years and Kerala.

"You know Malayalam then?" With a smile, Kiran enquired.

"A little like namaskaram," Grace retorted. "sugam anno." My speaking skills in Malayalam are not very good.

"Sis, your Malayalam is so sweet," said Kiran.

"She is not that much of sweet like you think, hehe," Jacob retorted.

Kiran laughed.

They arrived at the house.

Paradise was the name on the house's name board. It was a charming little house. The best part was the enormous garden. Lovely trees, vibrant flowers and an abundance of veggie plants.

Their house was a reflection of their optimistic outlook.

"Nice home and awesome garden," Kiran remarked.

"My husband deserves full credit," Grace retorted.

"I love gardening," Jacob stated with a smile. It provides some relief from the pressures of the IT industry."

Bro, so you are an IT professional?" Kiran inquired.

"Yes, the most stress-free job ever," Jacob answered ironically.

Laughing, Kiran enquired, "What about you, sis?"

"Well, I was a physics teacher, but I resigned," Grace answered. Right now, I work as a baker.

"My wife is the famous baker in Bangalore." Jacob retorted.

Grace smiled back and said, "I'm not that famous. On Instagram, I have a page. For God's sake, people place orders.

"Well, we didn't even enter our home. Welcome to our lovely home, guests," said Jacob.

Olivia excitedly clapped her hands.

"Sit down," Grace requested as they walked in.

Sheetal sat on the sofa with Kiran. Grace sat on the other chair, and Jacob sat on the one with Olivia on his lap.

"What you guys are doing?" inquired Jacob.

"I am an advocate," Kiran answered.

"I had expected it because of your talking style," Grace remarked.

Kiran chuckled.

What are you doing, Sheetal? Grace inquired.

"I am working as a cashier in a bank," Sheetal replied.

"Oh, I see, it sounds like an exhausting position." was Jacob's reply.

Sheetal agreed.

Olivia gave Kiran a teddy bear that she had taken.

"She liked you," Jacob shot back. She gifted her doll for that reason.

"So sweet," Kiran said with a smile.

"Well, how do you know each other?" inquired Grace. Friends?"

Sheetal and Kiran glared at one another.

In response, Kiran said, "We are just travel companions."

"Oh, I see," was Jacob's reply.

Kiran went on, "Well, I scheduled a trip with my travel companion, but his mother's illness prevented him from coming. We decided to travel together after I unexpectedly met her in Munnar because I was so bored with travelling alone.

Grace said, "That's quite nice." I know you guys must be exhausted. We will prepare cool drinks within 5 minutes. Please keep an eye on Olivia.

"Sure" Kiran replied.

Sheetal whispered, "Why are you obsessed with the term 'Travel Companions'?" as Jacob and Grace entered the kitchen.

"Then what is the relationship between us?"

Sheetal was at a loss for words.

"I can't consider you a friend," Kiran answered. Since you don't treat me well, I can't claim you're a stranger. Finally, "Travel Companion" is a suitable choice.

Sheetal commented, "Whatever."

A pair of juice glasses were served by Jacob and Grace.

After they had a drink, Kiran said, "Thank you."

There's no need for formality, Grace retorted.

Kiran grinned.

In response, Jacob said, "Well, these two rooms."

"You guys can stay in one room, and we ladies will stay in one," Grace answered. Alright?

Jacob gave a thumbs up.

"Go get yourself refreshed, and we'll get dinner ready. Grace recommended.

After gathering their belongings, they each walked to their room.

A few hours later, Jacob declared, "Supper is ready."

All of them are seated at the table. They got their meal going.

Kiran inquired, "So, did you choose to have an arranged marriage or was it based on love?" while she was eating.

Grace enquired, "What are your thoughts?"

"Love marriage?" Kiran responded.

"Exactly," was Jacob's response.

Kiran retorted, "Wow, tell me the story."

Jacob laughed and said, "It's a simple story. Our familiarity with each other stems from our childhood. We both went to the same church, and we both had feelings for each other. We didn't invest time that much like we don't usually didn't talk much. We met every Sunday, that's it."

Kiran was curious to know. Sheetal was paying attention, but not that much of the curious.

Grace continued, "We had a plan. Initially, we need to become financially independent and marry. We thought that our family would accept our love."

"Then?" inquired Kiran.

"Her family wanted a rich son-in-law, but my family was ready to accept her," Jacob stated. In addition, my family was not as wealthy as hers. They even arranged her engagement with an affluent man."

"Fortunately, we both had jobs at that time," Grace remarked. We were forced to elope and legally register our union. I was 24, and he was 25 at the time.

"We went to my home, but my family's reaction was shocking," Jacob retorted. They were upset with me because I had married before my sister, not because I had sought refuge from them. According to them, I had destroyed the family's dignity."

"Bro, this is your simple story," Kiran remarked. Sounds like a film.

"We both had begun our life without savings," Grace remarked with a giggle. Jacob had to give up everything, including his beloved bike.

"Fortunately, it was sold to one of my friends, and I bought it later," Jacob retorted. Grace's willingness to step outside of her comfort zone for me is largely responsible for our marriage.

Kiran said, "That's sweet."

To which Jacob answered, "Exactly. That's her most adorable quality.

"His love and presence were priceless," Grace answered. I am delighted to be with him for the rest of my life.

"You are a living example of true love," Kiran retorted. It is uncommon to come across a pair like this in this generation.

"Anyway, it wasn't easy for us," Jacob remarked. After much hardship, our family finally welcomed us.

"Wow," Kiran exclaimed.

Everybody consumed their meal.

"No need, dear, we will wash it," Grace answered as Sheetal took her plate.

"I usually do it," Sheetal responded.

"Never mind, you are our guests," Grace shot back.

Grace took the plate from Sheetal.

One hour later, Jacob announced, "It's ten o'clock now." I want to get up early because I know you people must be tired.

Indeed, we may go and sleep, Kiran replied.

Jacob waved his hand at Grace. She gestured a flying kiss. Jacob caught the kiss. Olivia was smiling, and she gave a goodnight kiss to her dad.

Kiran wished Sheetal a good night.

Sheetal said good night in response.

CHAPTER XII

THE CONFESSION

Kiran and Jacob slept easily together in the same bed.

Grace tried telling Olivia a story to put her to sleep.

Olivia fell asleep a short while later.

Grace invited Sheetal to come sleep here. "Here's to hoping we can all get used to it. This bed is fairly spacious.

"With a glance at Olivia, Sheetal sat on the bed.

"She will be the most silent and obedient kid ever when she sleeps," Grace went on.

Drawing a long breath, Sheetal answered, "Well, I know you may notice that I am not interacting with you guys like Kiran does. That does not imply that I am enraged or hateful. It's who I am."

"I know it because I have a little sister whose character is exactly like you," Grace added with a smile. Do you also have siblings?"

"Yes, an elder sister," Sheetal answered.

Grace enquired, "What is she doing?"

"She left me alone in this world," Sheetal said, her eyes welling with tears.

Grace inquired, "What happened to her?"

Sheetal continued, "It was discovered that she had an uncommon medical condition during her time as a college student, which required surgery." The surgeon suggested that she have surgery. Even though the costs were high, our parents had made some sort of arrangement. She recovered after the procedure and resumed her regular life. After graduating, she established her financial independence. However, she passed away after fainting one day."

Grace's eyes had also filled with tears.

Sheetal went on, "The world was changing around me after her death. For me, everyone gradually became unfamiliar, even my parents. Despite their recovery, I am unable to go past my loss. They always told me to forget about it and concentrate on myself when I confided in them about my pain. They were impatient and would not listen to me."

"See, I had very long and thick hair, which was the epitome of my sister's care and my happiness," Sheetal remarked, touching her hair.

"I even cut it completely and never allowed my hair to grow." I have been living the same miserable existence for almost ten years, and I have never wanted to escape from it. I even lost track of how to express my feelings."

Grace said, "You can express all your worries and grief to me," and held out a tissue. Consider me as your sister."

Sheetal hugged and replied, "You know, I am speaking to somebody like this after a long time. Just to pay back the loans, I had to live there for a decade. I paid it back and deposited the financial security for my parents. I could find no purpose in life. That's why I choose to travel. I had even tried suicide once, but it didn't work out."

Grace answered, "Child, ending your life is not an excellent plan. Everyone experiences hardships. People often have a misconception."

After wiping away her tears, Sheetal enquired, "What's that?"

"I am the only one going through an extremely miserable situation," Grace retorted.

Sheetal was clueless.

Grace continued, "No one is free from worries. Everybody has it. However, people approach it in different ways. For instance, although they don't talk about it, your parents had also suffered from the loss of their beloved daughter. Imagine what would happen if everyone believed that they would all end their lives by suicide. There would not be a single person left behind. And listen—remember your sister? She battled her illness. After graduating, she made an income.

Sheetal asked, "Am I a coward?

"No, you are not a coward, but you forgot to find happiness and wasted your years," Grace said, giving Sheetal a pat on the shoulder.

Grace enquired." Did you believe that your sister would be happy with the way you are living?"

"No, definitely," Sheetal replied.

And Grace responded, "That's it. Anyway, I wanna share something."

Sheetal replied, "Yeah."

Grace replied, "As you know, neither of our families accepted our marriage. There was a single reason which was money. I don't say money is nothing, but it is not everything. We had to deal with the dark side of life after marriage. Jacob and I both found it difficult to live our daily lives. Although we never asked for help from our relatives, they used us to suffer. They once even forgot that we are their children."

"I got pregnant after two years of our marriage," Grace said, her voice cracking. "We were delighted. When parents become grandparents, they usually forget all of their rivalry. Even my mother didn't come to meet me here. The only person who supported me from my family was my sister. Regretfully, the abortion resulted in the demise of my baby."

Sheetal replied, "Sis, don't cry."

Grace responded, "My parents' comments caused the most excruciating pain. They recently declared that God will punish us by taking our child. Following that event, we both started over in life. We desired to live in this world with pride and independence from our parents. We began to make plans to finish things, like purchasing a house and a car. These were our aims accomplished, this house and this car. I hope we can add one more floor in three years.

Sheetal gave a clap.

Grace answered, "Yes, these are all our blood, sweat, and tears. My sister informed me one day that my dad had been in an accident. I had no intention to meet him. However, Jacob made me go because they are our parents. Even though they were neglected, we will never forget them. We visited them.

"Then what happened?" Sheetal enquired.

Grace retorted, "I noticed my mom crying and contacting relatives when I came to visit him. That's when I understood my dad had given his savings to my relatives as debt. He believed his relatives would pay it forward. However, he was deceived. The majority of the wealth he had earned was lost. He attempted to end his life by causing an accident. My mother had requested all relatives for financial support. Since my sister was a trainee, she could not afford to cover all of the expenses. None of our family offered assistance."

"Did you help them?" inquired Sheetal.

Grace replied "Yes, we had a savings account saved for our future child. We had spent that money without giving it any thought. My dad's surgery was successful, and he recovered fully. Furthermore, a coincidence occurred."

"What was that?" asked Sheetal.

"My father-in-law was the one who had brought my dad to the hospital," Grace said.

Wow, Sheetal retorted.

"Yes, we were all shocked to see him in the hospital. He extended an embrace to my husband. Jesus had finally brought us together. And eight years into our marriage, I got pregnant again. This time, the doctor suggested I should quit my teaching profession. I disliked being dependent on my spouse since it would put further strain on him. Before getting married, I studied baking; therefore I decided to launch a baking business. It wasn't easy at first, but things got better.

"You are such an inspiring lady," Sheetal said.

"I shared my life story to make you realise that you need to live the life," Grace retorted.

Sheetal answered, "I appreciate it."

Never mind, Grace remarked. What would happen, therefore, if Olivia wakes to find these mature women weeping more than she does?"

They both chuckled.

Grace went on, "Well, it's 12:30 now. We must get some rest. Good night."

"Good night," Sheetal shot back.

She looked at Grace and gave her life another thought. For Sheetal, the night marked the brightest day in ten years.

CHAPTER XIII

AN EMOTIONAL ROLLERCOASTER

When Kiran awoke, he looked at the time.

It was 12:30 PM when he yelled, not expecting to be able to sleep for so long. He wasn't even certain of the location.

When he got to the living room, he noticed Olivia watching a cartoon. He was able to recall everything. Upon entering the kitchen, he noticed Sheetal and Grace.

Grace asked, "Why are you so early?" with a smile.

Kiran chuckled and apologised, asking, "Where's Jacob, bro?"

"He headed to the office", Grace said.

Sheetal asked, "What are you planning to do today?"Kiran said, "I'm not sure."

"For real?" Sheetal asked in reply.

Grace stated, "He still feels sleepy. Kiran, take a moment to recharge."

Kiran gave a thumbs up and went.

It took him a few minutes to arrive.

It's time for lunch, Grace declared.

The group gathered around the dining table.

"How was your sleep here, Kiran?" Grace inquired.

"It was so nice. I was fatigued from the journey. How was yours, Sheetal?" Kiran retorted.

Sheetal answered, "Yes, me too. I was also a late riser.

Olivia was being fed by Grace.

"Can we go to Wonderla, Sheetal?" asked Kiran.

Sheetal replied, "Okay."

Grace remarked, "I want to deliver a cake to a nearby home, which is near Wonderla so I'll drop you guys off."

"Sis, can you come with us?" inquired Sheetal.

Sheetal began to appear a little kinder, which startled Kiran a little.

"Oh, I can't, because I have orders. It's a holiday tomorrow, so don't worry, Jacob has suggested one plan." Grace answered.

Kiran and Sheetal became thrilled. "WHAT IS THE PLAN?" they all questioned at once.

Grace answered, "You look as happy as Olivia did when I gave her favourite candy, haha. We could have a picnic."

"That's a great idea," Kiran said.

"Yes, it is," Sheetal answered.

They consumed their food.

"Sis, I'll take care of the dishes since you and Olivia need to get ready," Kiran remarked.

Sheetal must also be ready. For the trip, I am already ready.

Grace replied, "No need. You are our guests."

Kiran replied, "You had said no formalities. Then what?"

"All right, I'm not as good at arguing as you are," Grace said and went.

Grace said, "I hope everyone is ready," a few minutes later.

They all got into the car after Grace locked the main door of the house.

"Olivia, you got a special seat," said Kiran.

Olivia chuckled.

Grace dropped Kiran and Sheetal while operating the vehicle. Grace waved her hands and said, "Travel companions, enjoy your day."Olivia waved her tiny hand as well.

With a smile, Kiran and Sheetal gestured with their hands.

"We need to buy t-shirts from that shop," Kiran remarked.

Sheetal gave a nod.

There was a street vendor who was selling T-shirts of different colours.

"Which t-shirt does you want, sir and madam?" the salesman inquired.

They were examining the T-shirts closely.

Sheetal selected a blue T-shirt, whereas Kiran went for a red one. They purchased it. The T-shirts came in various colours, but they shared the same design.

They went through Wonderla's front gate.

"I guess we are lucky enough to come in November," Kiran exclaimed.

"Why?" Sheetal questioned.

"Because Wonderla is typically crowded with people," he said. Things are okay today.

"Come on, we can enjoy," Kiran remarked, pointing to a ride.

Seat belts were tied by them.

Kiran pocketed his spectacles. The ride spun around. When it started, everyone burst into joyful shouts.

Kiran was surprised by Sheetal's response. She was yelling with joy. Given her previous actions, he never would have predicted this type of behaviour from her.

"We can go on that octopus ride," Sheetal responded after the ride was over.

Kiran gave a nod. His expression was bewilderment.

After the ride, Sheetal remarked, "Wow, I liked it".They rode the rollercoaster after that. They were seated in one row together. Sheetal had a hint of worry on her face.

"Are you afraid?" inquired Kiran.

"Not that much, but still," said Sheetal.

"Don't worry, just enjoy it," Kiran urged.

The roller coaster began to accelerate.

They both shut their eyes. Their emotions changed more quickly than the rollercoaster.

Screaming, fear, excitement, tension, and fun, etc.

After the ride, Kiran replied, "I now understand why it is named rollercoaster. I could shift across emotions more quickly than an actor.

Sheetal remarked, "Indeed."

They captured a picture together.

And Sheetal said, "I am going to post it and I will add the caption "With my travel companion OK."

Kiran frowned and asked, "Are you teasing me?"

Sheetal asked, "Why?"

Kiran said, "Why are you stressing the word "Travel companion'?

Sheetal replied, "Then what should I say?"

"Whatever," Kiran sighed.

And he continued, "You had transformed in just one day, by the way. The Sheetal I had met a few days prior was reticent, disliked jokes, and wouldn't even engage in conversation with people. You are having fun on the rides today and have started interacting with me more."

In response, Sheetal said, "Lol, people will change. And if you want to go on the water rides, we're already running late. Come on, please.

They visited a water park and had fun at a variety of attractions.

"We are in our 30s and still enjoying like kids," Kiran remarked.

"How do you know I am 30 years old?" asked Sheetal.

"I thought you were 39 something," Kiran shot back.

In response, Sheetal said, "You are 45, correct?"

"No, I am just 30 years old," Kiran retorted.

Sheetal agreed by saying "Same."

They took the bus to Jacob and Grace's house after leaving Wonderla.

Grace gave them a warm welcome and some delicious teas.

CHAPTER XIV

A FUTURISTIC QUESTION

Grace enquired, "How was the experience?"

Kiran answered, "Tickets were expensive but worth the money. We had a lot of fun."

"I enjoyed it," Sheetal replied.

Jacob arrived.

Jacob said, "Guys, we need to talk about tomorrow's trip. I will come back after refreshing myself."

A short while later, Jacob arrived and sat down on the couch.

And he asked, "Guys, how about going to Mysore tomorrow?"

By exchanging glances, Kiran and Sheetal were able to determine each other's interests. They agreed.

"Could you please tell me about the places?" inquired Sheetal.

"Museum, Aquarium, Botanical Garden, etc." was Jacob's response.

"We need to start our journey from 7 AM," Grace retorted.

She glared at Kiran.

Remarking, "Don't worry, I will wake up," Kiran laughed.

After eating supper, they retired to bed.

Everyone except Olivia woke up early. Everyone was scrambling to prepare.

At last, everyone prepared and got into the car.

Olivia is sitting in the front seat alongside Jacob and Grace, while Kiran and Sheetal occupy the back seat.

They started their journey to Mysore.

"Bro, how much time would it take us to reach Mysore?" Kiran inquired.

Jacob replied, "I think 2-3 hours."

"I don't think it will take three hours because it will be almost two and a quarter hours, maybe," Grace remarked.

Grace had Olivia curled up on her lap.

"Well, we have plenty of time to talk," Kiran inquired. I'd like to learn more about your love story.

Jacob chuckled with Grace.

Grace replied, "Our love story is simple." However, I believed that we would unite together."

"I used to give her handwritten letters on her birthday, and she does the same," Jacob answered.

"I had preserved those," said Grace.

"Olivia will be happy to read her parent's love letters," Sheetal replied.

"I know it is a crazy question," Kiran asked. Nevertheless, asking. How will you feel if Olivia chooses the person she wants to marry?

Everyone chuckled.

"What kind of question is this?" Sheetal asked. She is only a young child.

Kiran commented, "I just asked a futuristic question. Avoid over-analysing."

"The problem is my overthinking, not your silly question," Sheetal replied.

With a frown, Kiran shot back, "Just take a joke as a joke."

Jacob said, "Calm down."

Olivia started to cry.

In response, Grace said, "Guys, you are behaving like kids."

Grace attempted to put Olivia to sleep.

Jacob answered back, "We will be the happiest parents if our daughter marries a man who truly loves and respects her."

Grace stated, "We will try to advise her that her choice is not good if she makes the wrong choice." She nevertheless has a blind love affair. Then there is nothing we can do. All we can do is watch as she experiences the consequences.

Kiran and Sheetal gave it a close listen.

"We will teach her about the importance of education and financial independence," Jacob retorted.

With a clap, Kiran said, "You are great."

"You are long-sighted parents, Sheetal retorted.

With a glance at Kiran, she apologised.

It's okay, Kiran said.

"Kiran, what is your marital status?" inquired Jacob.

Kiran answered with a giggle, "I am single and leading a peaceful life. Furthermore, why did you pose this query?"

"Nothing, I had just inquired," Jacob retorted. How are you doing, Sheetal?

Sheetal said, "I'm not married."

"Your parent didn't compel you, right?" Grace asked.

In response, Sheetal said, "No, they didn't."

"My parents won't force me to get married, but my younger brother always wants me to get married," Kiran replied.

Grace exclaimed, "What a lovely brother!"

"Yes, dear brother, he looked out for me because he wants to get married after my marriage," Kiran answered.

Everyone chuckled.

They arrived at Mysore after two hours.

CHAPTER XV

MYSORE

"Guys, we made it to our destination," Jacob said. Olivia raised a hand.

They reached Mysore palace.

They gathered the tickets. Olivia woke up from her sleep with a lot of energy. It brought her great joy to tour the palace.

Grace answered, "We must take off our sandals. It is safe to be kept in the cloakroom."

Taking off their sandals, they went inside.

The palace's designs, architecture, and treasures astounded them. Everything amazed them.

"Guys, this palace is a fusion of different styles like Indian, Arabic, Mughal, Roman, and Rajput architecture," Jacob remarked.

Sheetal answered, "Oh, I see. This explains why the palace appears so majestic."

"Look, that was known as Elephant entrance," Kiran replied, pointing.

And Sheetal said, "What?"

Olivia said "Elephant" commented

"Yes, Sheetal," Grace replied.

Kiran said, glancing at Sheetal in response, "This used to be the entrance where elephants used to enter. And because of this, I've heard a rumour that the people of this country used to be terrified of the elephants that used to attack them. One elephant's head is visible where Tipu Sultan severed the heads of the elephants. He did this to demonstrate that his subjects' lives were secure under his care."

"Elephant," said Olivia.

Sheetal laughed, saying, "What a terrifying tale!"

Kiran let out a sigh.

In the hallways, they noticed stunning drawings. Seeing the 2D and 3D paintings amazed everyone.

Then they saw the marriage hall, which was shaped like an octagon.

They spotted numerous portraits of various kings as they moved into the next area.

"I just admired the talent of our ancestors," Kiran said.

That's true, Jacob answered.

They finished their tour of the Mysore Palace.

"I am so happy to visit here as a humanities student, his eyes glimmering. How creative!" Kiran said.

"Thank you so much for taking us here," Sheetal responded.

"Never mind, it's time for lunch now. We just finished our early-morning breakfast." Grace replied.

They had their lunch at a restaurant.

They arrived at Aqua World in Mysore. It was a zoo under the sea. They accepted tickets.

Olivia was ecstatic to witness the underwater zoo's vibrant atmosphere.

They observed a wide range of aquatic creatures, including turtles, starfish, and eels.

After completing the first floor, they made their way to the lower level.

"Olivia, that is a lionfish," Grace replied, pointing to one fish.

"LIONFISH," Olivia repeated as her eyes grew wide.

Jacob chuckled. "These fish look so beautiful," Grace said.

They noticed many fish as they passed. For a little while, they forgot about their stresses and worries. The Underwater Aquarium was magnificent.

At last, their visits came to an end.

Grace inquired, "How was your experience? Because of lack of time, we only visit two locations. I hope it was enjoyable for you."

"It was awesome," Sheetal retorted.

"I liked it and I have one suggestion," Kiran remarked.

"Proceed," Jacob said.

"I know bro will be too tired to drive once again. I'm ready to drive, and if it's okay with you, sis and baby can relax as well." Kiran retorted.

As Jacob put it, "You're right. It will be difficult for you to use Google Maps alone, but I'm tired.

"I will help him," was Sheetal's response.

"Guys, remember to buy parcels to eat," Grace remarked.

Kiran answered, "All right, any preferences?"

"Anything, but we're all hungry enough," Grace retorted.

"Don't worry, I will buy accordingly," Kiran retorted.

Kiran and Sheetal occupied the front seats, while Jacob and Grace took their places in the back seats.

Kiran started to drive, and Sheetal helped him by telling him the correct routes.

Jacob, Grace, and Olivia fell asleep deeply after thirty minutes.

"They are sleeping peacefully," Kiran stated in an elegant voice.

Sheetal gave a nod.

"They trust us so much. That explains why they are sleeping peacefully." Kiran said.

Sheetal answered, "That's true."

Kiran replied, "They have a good heart."

"Yes, they have," Sheetal responded. And what plans do you have for tomorrow?

"Not yet," Kiran retorted.

Well, what about going on a ship journey?" Sheetal countered.

"Ship journey on sea waters!" Kiran exclaimed. It would be better if we tried any other place.

"This is so unfair," shouted Sheetal. I agree with any locations you recommend, but when I make a suggestion, you just deny it."

Kiran answered, "Please don't scream. I'm driving and they're sleeping. Alright, I'll be there."

At last, they arrived at the house.

CHAPTER XVI

THE VOYAGE

The following morning, everyone woke up with a smile on their faces. They all enjoyed the day out. Grace was preparing breakfast as Jacob was busy getting ready.

Sheetal and Kiran dressed. They also brought their backpacks.

"Are you going without giving a proper farewell?" Grace inquired.

"No, sis, we are only going for one day," Sheetal retorted. We have a ship voyage planned.

Jacob retorted, "It will be expensive."

"Not that much because we are not going for a long distance," Sheetal said.

Grace answered, "Kiran, that's fantastic. What's up with your fearful appearance?

"No, sis, I just thought about the journey," Kiran retorted. After the ride, we will meet. Goodbye. Olivia is where?

Grace stated, "She's asleep."

Kiran regarded her, admiring her cuteness. "My dear, uncle and aunt will be back soon." He gave her a gentle head pat.

"You would also have a baby like her if you had married at the right age," Jacob remarked.

Kiran clasped his hands and begged him not to behave like his little brother.

Everyone chuckled. "Sis and bro, we can meet later," Sheetal remarked.

Beaming, she took Grace's hands in hers.

Grace replied, "Bon voyage."

They took a bus to their destination. After making the payment, they boarded the ship. Though the ship was large, there were many passengers on board.

They made their way to the ship's upper deck.

They set out on their journey.

Kiran's discomfort with this excursion was the reason he wasn't feeling well.

"This reminds me of the Titanic," Sheetal remarked.

Kiran gave a nod.

When Sheetal saw his peculiar behaviour, she asked, "Are you mimicking me? Typically, you speak a lot and poetically describe the beauty of places.

"I am uncomfortable with this journey," Kiran retorted. I'm worn out.

Sheetal offered a lemon, saying, "You might feel better if you smell this."

"Finally, you proved you are also a human being," Kiran remarked while smelling the lemon.

"So you assumed I was an alien?" Sheetal retorted.

"You were a virago and laconic woman when I met," Kiran retorted. A few things about your behaviour have changed. However, you must develop into a human being.

"I am not a chatterbox unlike you," Sheetal responded.

Suddenly, people were screaming beneath the ship's ground floor. They made an effort to figure out what was going on there.

They discovered that a small group of pirates had taken control of the ship and had armed themselves with regular folk. Staying on the ship was not safe.

There were just Kiran and Sheetal on the upper floor.

Kiran grabbed his phone and called the police to report this.

"Remaining here is not safe," whispered Sheetal. Are you able to swim?

Kiran answered, "Yeah, but."

The robbers became aware of them. "See, that guy told the police about us."

"Kill him." The bandits revealed.

Sheetal gave him a blank look and gestured for him to leap. They dive with their luggage.

"We lost them, nonsense, a robber," said. Either way, they will die. Fools.

They kept swimming till they came to land. It was an island.

They inhaled deeply while resting on the sand.

Kiran was on his feet. He wandered around the island to see whether anyone was human. His heartbeat was audible to him.

They found themselves trapped on an unidentified island.

Sheetal remained on the sandy ground. "Fortunately, we are safe from those pirates," she declared.

Kiran stared at Sheetal, his cheeks turning redder. His strange attitude confused her.

Kiran cried out, "SAFE? AN UNKNOWN ISLAND IS THIS. I am aware that you are tired of your life. "YOU DRAG ME ALSO?"

Sheetal arose to her feet and said, "Pardon me."

"YOU HAD TRIED TO COMMIT SUICIDE IN MUNNAR," Kiran yelled out, closing his eyes in rage. I lied about the climate condition because I knew it. I don't want to become suspicious of your suicide. Simply put, if you want to die, stay on this island. I desire to survive.

Sheetal answered, "You're correct. I had attempted suicide, but I no longer intended to do it. What therefore ought to be required of me? They might kill you because you told the police.

Kiran shot back, "How are we going to survive here?"

"I hope ships may come to rescue us," Sheetal sighed.

Laughing, Kiran said, "Yes, like films, right?"

He looked at his phone. Fortunately, it wasn't wet because, in a rush, he covered it with a plastic wrap, and Sheetal did the same.

"NO RANGE," Kiran yelled.

Sheetal whispered, "Calm down. You at least have your glasses and phone.

Gazing at her, Kiran uttered, "Calm down. How can you stay calm like this? HOW WILL WE GET FOOD AND WATER?"

"Well, I have two bottles of cool drinks and mineral water," Sheetal retorted. If the supply of mineral water runs out, we can drink rainfall.

"Rain is your maternal uncle?" Kiran asked.

Sheetal chuckled.

Kiran asked, "Are you insane? You are completely normal, even though you are stuck on an island. You have a limited supply of chilled drink bottles. When it's done, what will we do?"

Sheetal could take no more of Kiran's blabbering.

"Then you kill and eat my flesh to rid yourself of your hunger," Sheetal remarked.

Kiran stared at her and said, "I will do it, but I am not a dog to eat the bones. There is no flesh on your body."

Sheetal became wild. She rushed after him to beat him. Kiran chuckled and took off running.

A tree was in front of Kiran's eyes. There were many ripe mangoes in the mango tree.

"There are enough mangos to eat," Sheetal retorted. There are several more mango trees, as you can see.

Mangoes with yellow flesh were harvested from trees.

They arrived at the island in the evening. They may have been afraid that this was where they would pass away, so they were not as hungry as they would have been on other days.

CHAPTER XVII

TALKING

They could hear the melody of crickets in the night. They lay on the beach and ate mangos.

Sufficient space separated them.

They were looking up at the moon.

For them, the sole source of illumination was the moon. They lost themselves in contemplation.

Sand on the floor caused agony in Kiran's neck. He grabbed the head pillow and threw a head pillow towards Sheetal.

"That's it. It won't strain your neck," Kiran retorted.

Sheetal expressed gratitude.

Kiran grabbed his phone and took a selfie.

Sheetal inquired, "Capturing memories right?"

"Yes, there is no grantee; I will wake up tomorrow," Kiran remarked.

Sheetal remarked, "Are you scared of wild animals? I don't believe any wild creatures exist here. My observations lead me to believe that it must be a remote island. I'm hoping boats or ships could arrive to save us."

"If they didn't come, what would you do?" Kiran shot back.

Sheetal retorted, "I'm not sure. Let's put those out of our minds. Please take a picture of me."

They snapped a photo together after Kiran captured her picture.Sheetal was a little afraid as well, but she kept it to herself for fear of upsetting Kiran as well. But she had thought someone might save them.

"*Lying on the sandy floor with seawater on four sides and watching the moon is a very good experience,*" Kiran remarked.

"That's true,' Sheetal remarked, gazing at the moon.

"*An authentic fusion of natural elements*", added Kiran.

They grinned. They were bestowed with the soft breeze.

"Why did you try to commit suicide back then?" Kiran questioned.

With laughter, Sheetal answered, "Nothing. There was no reason for me to live.

"Oh really? You got fed up with your life?" Kiran retorted.

"Yes," she answered.

"See, we had travelled together for almost five days, but I never irritated you by asking about your life," Kiran inquired. However, I'm curious now because I just need to divert my attention from my thoughts to avoid becoming disturbed by our circumstances and overthinking them.

"You wanna know about my life, right?" inquired Sheetal.

"Yes," Kiran replied.

"I lead a normal life with my parents and my elder sister," Sheetal retorted. She was my support system, similar to my parents. In my 30-year life, I have never met someone who loves and takes care of me as much as she does.

"So, you lost her?" Kiran asked.

Shocked, Sheetal enquired, "How do you know it?"

"I just predicted," Kiran retorted. You once mentioned that your sister used to make noodles, but you chose to dismiss my questions about her. I had noticed the expressions on your face.

"You observe your surroundings a lot, right?" Sheetal retorted.

"As an advocate, observation is also a crucial skill," Kiran replied.

"You are right, I lost her," Sheetal retorted. Her unusual condition was identified by the doctors. The surgeon recommended surgery. My parents took out loans to raise the money, even though it was expensive. The procedure went well. She even worked after earning her degree, but she passed away suddenly.

She wiped her eyes, tears welling up in them.

"Perhaps that incident changed you right?" Kiran asked.

"Yeah, after her dead, I lost my faith in god and connection with everyone around me," Sheetal admitted. My sister used to style my long, thick hair, but I chopped it off, and I've stuck with the same look ever since.

"Tomboy hairstyle, you just forgot about yourself lol," Kiran replied.

Sheetal agreed: "You're correct. My sole goal was to get out of the financial trap. A private bank hired me to work as a cashier. I set my parents a fixed account and paid back the loans after years of diligent work.

"You love your parents, but don't express that," Kiran added with a clap.

"I don't know how to express my emotions to anyone," Sheetal retorted. I was virago and laconic, like you said. My goals accomplished, I felt empty. I had money set up for myself. I made the decision to use that money for a solitary journey.

"Good, and you must have a lot of haters," Kiran retorted.

That's true, Sheetal remarked with a laugh. I never thought I would be with a travel companion.

"My bad luck," Kiran muttered.

Sheetal asked, "What did you say?"

"Nothing, I just had a sneeze," Kiran retorted.

Sheetal became aware of his remarks. She was only acting.

"Probably Grace sis, changed your mentality right," Kiran retorted.

"Yes, I felt like she is my sister," Sheetal retorted.

"I guess that because your character had changed after visiting them," Kiran remarked.

"Well, I shared about my life; now talk about your life," Sheetal remarked.

"My family consists of me, my wonderful dad, my sweet mom, and my crazy brother," Kiran stated.

"You had described your parents on good terms, so why did you call your bro crazy?" Sheetal laughed.

"Because he is crazy," Kiran retorted. I thought of him as my enemy from a previous life at times. You know what, one day when I was a school student, a female classmate phoned me with a question about our group assignment. My parents were told by this guy that she was my girlfriend. And my parents thought it was true.

I knew how hard I had tried to persuade them that it was incorrect.

Sheetal laughed in response.

"Have you ever fallen in love with someone?" Kiran said.

"Nobody approached me and I don't approach anyone," Sheetal retorted.

"That's a cool response," Kiran said.

And Sheetal inquired, "How about you?"

Smiling, Kiran stood up and replied, "Yes."

Nice, said Sheetal as she stood up as well. Share your tale of love.

"I was afraid to love someone because if I love someone sincerely, I will get attached to them," Kiran remarked, giving the moon a fierce look. Since everyone thought me as a joke, I didn't have any relationships in school. I gave my work a lot of attention. I got an admission to a government law college. My friends were mostly in relationships, but I was single. And I never imagined that I would also acquire a girlfriend.

Inquiring, "Who is she?" Sheetal asked.

Kiran answered, "Her name was Kiara." She was a student in my class. Being an ambivert, she aspired to concentrate on her work. She had proposed to me. And I didn't know if I should accept it or reject it. My friends said that I am fortunate as they work hard to get a girlfriend. She had proposed to me, in my instance. There was nothing for me to do. I agreed to that.

Then, Sheetal questioned.

"We were different from every other couple on campus," Kiran went on. We don't waste time visiting movie theatres or ice cream shops. Together, we studied in libraries. She wanted to be a company secretary, and I wanted to be a Munsiff Magistrate. Although we often discussed movies and campus activities, our goals took up much of our conversation.

Sheetal said, "Oh, I see."

"Most of my friends' relationships had broken, and they even started new relationships," Kiran remarked with a smile. My friends used to tell me how great and healthy our relationship was. She was even familiar to my family. We intended to tie the knot once we had both achieved our ambitions.

Kiran said nothing but smiled while staring at the moon.

"Go ahead," Sheetal replied.

Kiran took off his glasses. Sheetal was waiting for his response with patience.

Kiran answered, "We had a farewell after our final exam of the semester. She came up to me after the programme and said, 'We can end our relationship because college life ended'."

Sheetal merely glanced back, saying, "What?"

With a nod, Kiran showed that he was perplexed. She just said, "Break up," and left. A few of my pals suggested that it had to be a joke. She never answered the phone when I tried to reach her.

"What was the reason for your breakup?" inquired Sheetal.

"I asked her friend and her friend's answer was shocking," Kiran retorted. Kiara did not take meseriously. I was just a tutor.

"Are you sure?" Sheetal said in response.

"She needed an unpaid tutor to help her studies, and she wanted a boyfriend because all of her friends had," Kiran shot back with a smile.

Tears clouded Kiran's eyes as he continued, "She was everything to me." In my fantasy, she would lead a life with me and we would overcome our dreams. This happened after five years of dating without any significant arguments.

Puzzlement crossed Sheetal's face. She was at a loss about how to comfort him.

"And she caused a heartbreak just two days before my Munsiff Magistrate prelims exam. I wasn't able to attend the exam," Kiran shot back.

Sheetal shouted back, "Oh my God!"

"This is where the fun starts," Kiran remarked. My father had just one addiction. He was a drunkard. Exactly a day after the heartbreak my dad was diagnosed with liver cirrhosis for his treatment, I needed to find money. Our family belonged to the middle class. We had a difficult time raising so much money. My mom owned a stitching shop, and my dad worked as a postmaster.

His sons were students. Furthermore, my brother needed money to be enrolled. He cracked the NEET examination.

"How do you manage all of this?" Sheetal asked curiously.

"I could commit suicide and easily escape from this world," Kiran retorted. However, if I did, I would be making a grave mistake for me and my family. I had decided to face it instead of running away.

Sheetal enquired, "So what happened?"

"The only option available to me after enrollment was to work as a junior advocate under a senior advocate," Kiran said. For me, it wasn't simple. My senior was a man of a brief rage and perfection. He didn't have to hear my side of the story and accused me for the mistakes I never did. Furthermore, my pay was insufficient to keep us afloat. I had a lot of responsibilities.

"How old were you back then?" Sheetal inquired."

"I guess 24 years," Kiran remarked. I began going to a restaurant in the evenings for vessel cleaning. My parents had worked hard to perceive me as an advocate, therefore I never told them about my employment. Though I understood that each work has its dignity, my parents could not endure this.

Sheetal answered, "Well, I see."

"I used to lie I had extra work in my senior's office," Kiran went on. I was going through a tough time during those days. I was prepared to smile at those. I began to discover joy in the little things.

Sheetal answered, "You are amazing."

"One day, my family and I went to a marriage function," Kiran said, smiled. The man who owned the hotel where I was employed was my father's childhood buddy.

She said, "Oh my God."

Indeed, what a coincidence, Kiran retorted. I met him through my father. He gave a nod, although he withheld anything from my dad. That makes me happy for him. He came to talk to me on his own. He believed that by claiming to be an advocate, and was lying to my parents. I was honest when I said it.

"You had convinced him, right?" inquired Sheetal.

"He wasn't ready to trust me," Kiran retorted. After checking up on me, he realised that I was correct. He even seated for one hearing of me in the court.He was deeply impressed by my skills in my profession. For me, he was an angel—an angel with a long beard.

Sheetal said, "I'm not sure I get it."

In response, Kiran said, "He suggested me to his acquaintances who had cases, but he had few property matters himself. I was promoted from vessel cleaner to his advocate by him.

Wow, Sheetal retorted.

"Then, gradually, I started to earn more," Kiran stated. At last, I paid back my loans. My brother graduated in a few years and began his medical career. My senior did not object to me accepting cases, even though he was aware of them. I used to put money aside for travel. It had finally occurred. In any case, I planned to take a two-week leave of absence; therefore I had resigned from my senior advocate's firm.

Inquiring, "What is your next plan?" Sheetal.

In response, Kiran said, "I am not sure enough to practise as an independent advocate. Although they require a great deal of experience, I believe I should go to interviews with cooperating companies as a legal counsellor or consultant. Whatever, all I have to do is enjoy my holidays. I have no idea if I will make it out of this island alive.

"I firmly believe that some ship or boat will save us," Sheetal retorted.

"I don't wanna think about that," Kiran retorted.

"Then you don't need to think about this," Sheetal remarked. I have heard that guys who have broken will begin to hate women. Is that accurate?

"After the breakup, I never hated whole women as some immature people do," Kiran retorted. I have female friends too. Somehow, they resembled my sisters. Unlike me, the majority of them got married and had children. To be very honest, both men and women who are my friends have improved the quality of my existence. And my rambunctious brother as well. Although we argue frequently, he was supportive at the time.

"You never had any relationship after Kiara?" Sheetal inquired.

Kiran answered, "No, I'm not sure." I don't trust people very often, but I really thought Kiara would be in my life forever. I wasn't in a relationship for almost six years. I'm not sure what has happened to me. My brother is pressuring me to tie the knot so he can find a spouse. I'm sure I'll talk to my parents after this trip, find the ideal woman for him, and set up the marriage.

"I never had expected such a backstory from you," Sheetal retorted.

With a smile, Kiran remarked, "It sounds like you felt bored."

In response, Sheetal said, "No, it was interesting." I am grateful that you are happier than I am.

"Your life has not ended," Kiran replied. And you have too much optimism when you are trapped on this island. Anyhow, have a good evening. Additionally, remember to utilise a head pillow.

Goodnight, Sheetal said, yawning.

CHAPTER XVIII

A SWEET FAREWELL

It was midday, yet two of our travel companions remained sleeping on the sandy floor. They had recently fallen asleep after spending the night sharing their life stories. The island has such a tranquil feeling.

Sheetal heard an odd noise. She awoke, glaring at the ocean. She believed it to be a dream. There was a ship in the water.

Sheetal was astonished to see the ship.

She cried out, "KIRAN"

Kiran continued to relish his slumber. She walked up to him and gave him a shake on the shoulder.

"THE SHIP IS HERE, KIRAN."

When Kiran awoke, his mouth fell open as he questioned, "ARE YOU SURE?"

"PLEASE GET UP AND WE NEED TO ASK HELP FROM HIM," Sheetal retorted.

Rising, Kiran seized his jacket and turned it around. With haste, Sheetal grabbed one of her blankets and turned around.

They cried out, "PLEASE HELP US!"

A man on board noticed them after a few minutes and told a man who appeared to be the boss. The ship gradually changed course and approached them.

With a stare, Kiran and Sheetal chuckled at one another. As a sign of their collective survival, they lifted their hands together.

It was a fishing ship. This ship belonged to a middle-aged man named Rafeek.

With a sincere smile, Rafeeq uttered the words "Children, don't need to worry, you can enter my ship" in Tamil. You can rely on us.

Our travel companions had brought their backpacks on board and entered in the ship.

In the large net spread out across the ship's floor, they observed much-quivering fishes.

"How did you guys get trapped there?" asked Rafeek.

Kiran and Sheetal narrated the entire story

"I heard the news that the police captured the pirates," stated Rafeek. Fortunately, Abu noticed you and told me that two folks need our assistance. You two are from Kerala, right?

"Yes," Kiran inquired. Tamil is understandable to us.

"I am from Tamil Nadu and can understand Malayalam," Rafeek retorted.

They chuckled.

The ship arrived in the harbour.

"I cannot figure out how to express our gratitude to you for saving us," Sheetal retorted.

"No need for gratitude," was Rafeek's response. It is simply the bare minimum. If you two travelled with more caution, that would be beneficial. Though it may sound like cliched advice, you should nonetheless look out for yourself.

"Could you please give me your number?" Kiran enquired.

Rafeek shared his phone number.

They took a photo of the kind man, who was usually glowing with delight and bid him farewell. Sheetal was familiar with Jacob and Grace's address.

They took a cab and arrived at their house. Kiran pressed the entry bell.

Grace opened the door. She was taken aback upon seeing them.

"You guys said it was a one-day trip, and you didn't come back," she inquired. You remind me of my younger sister, Sheetal, and this is a bad habit. We assumed that you had returned to Kerala.

In response, Sheetal said, "An island trapped us."

Grace was taken aback.

They told the whole tale. Grace was sorry for them.

Kiran showed the photographs.

"This uncle is an incredible person," Grace commented. That there are people around the world like this makes me happy.

"Yeah," Kiran answered. When will Bro return from work? "He will come in the evening," Grace remarked. And what's your plan, guys?

"I am planning to go to Mumbai tomorrow," Kiran stated. Are you coming with me, Sheetal?

Sheetal answered, "Yeah."

"Now you guys become accurate travel companions," Grace retorted. There was a mocking tone in her voice.

"Where is Olivia?" inquired Kiran.

Grace answered, "Yes, she is asleep." Oh, I see. I want to create the cake's design. You people need to refresh.

The travel companions nodded.

Everyone was having dinner that night.

"So you guys are going to Mumbai by train tomorrow, right?" Jacob enquired.

"Yes, 23 hours," Kiran answered. It never occurred to me that Bangalore and Mumbai were so far apart.

Grace remarked, "Anyway, it must be difficult. It has to be a novel encounter.

Sheetal answered, "That is accurate."

"Guys, we will surely miss you," Jacob remarked.

Grace answered, "Yeah, we had a great time with you. And stay in contact at all times.

Kiran answered, "Certainly."

After eating supper, they retired to bed.

Kiran and Sheetal took their backpacks the following day.

"Jacob bro, could you please give me your number?" Kiran asked.

After giving it to her, Jacob said, "You can call me anytime you need any help."

Grace hugged Sheetal warmly and said, "I'm happy to have a sister like you." Additionally, remember to "like" the Instagram photos I make of my cakes.

Sheetal chuckled, tears welling up in her eyes. "Maybe I'm being too dramatic," she said.

Kiran told Olivia that her uncle was leaving for Mumbai.

Cutie, please try not to worry your parents about your mischievous actions.

Grinning, Olivia reached for Kiran's glasses.

Jacob answered, "What a well-behaved child! She was merely attempting to throw away your spectacles.

Everyone started laughing heartily.

The cab had pulled up outside the gate.

"Alright, guys, let's meet again," Grace said.

"Travel companions, enjoy your journey," Jacob retorted.

Olivia gave a little wave.

Kiran and Sheetal gestured with their hands and got into the car.

The travelling companions bonded strongly with them in a matter of days.

They were dropped off at the Bangalore railway station by the taxi.

CHAPTER XIX

IN THE TRAIN

They purchased bottles of mineral water and had breakfast.

A few days prior, Kiran had purchased train tickets online.

They entered the train and found their seats.

They opted to sit face-to-face to satisfy their shared preference for window seats.

"Our journey will begin in a few minutes," Kiran retorted.

Sheetal gave a nod.

The train moved forward. There weren't many passengers on the train; it was quite empty.

"I thought the train would be crowded," Sheetal remarked.

"Usually does and this route is so long and now it's not a vacation season," Kiran said.

Sheetal glanced out the window and nodded.

The phone rang for Kiran. He answered the phone.

"Hey, Mom."

"How are you doing?"

"I'm doing great."

"How is your journey progressing, then?"

"It's going great, and I'm currently travelling to Mumbai by train from Bangalore.

"Keerthan showed me a photo of a female with short hair and you. Is that you and your new friend?"

"No, she's my travel companion."

"Alright, care for her as well. Despite her smile, the image made me feel that she was depressed. That is the reason I told you what I did.

"Mum, when you turn from a tailor to a psychologist? What a smooth transition!"

"Take caution. Alright. Even if my son is thirty years old, I continue to possess counsel from you."

"And I am aware that you will precisely administer medication to your hubby while neglecting your own needs. You also need to look after your health."

"Alright, Mr Advocate."

"Goodbye, I'll speak with you later."

"Goodbye."

The call was cut off.

"She's so cute and innocent," Kiran retorted. My crazy brother likes to play practical jokes on her. However, she has outstanding money management abilities. Well, after speaking with my mother, I felt so calm.

Sheetal grinned.

In response, Kiran said, "What are you waiting for? Give your parents a call.

"Usually, I don't call them," Sheetal stated. Also not sure how to approach them.

Kiran chuckled and asked, "Why do you keep pushing them away?" They are not strangers; they are your parents. If you call them, they should be delighted. And if you give them a call, I'm pretty confident. You'll have conversation starters.

With a nervous smile, Sheetal questioned, "Are you sure?"

"Absolutely," Kiran responded.

Sheetal gave her mom a call.

"Hello, mom."

"Is Sheetal there?

"Yes, mom."

"Dear, what happens to you?"

"I just wanted to talk to you, Mom. Nothing else. It has been a while."

"I am happy that you spoke with us at last. We were rather concerned about you. We couldn't stand being apart from you." Her voice was trembling.

"Mum, are you crying?"

"NO, dear."

"Mom, I sincerely apologise for neglecting you and Dad." Sheetal broke down in tears.

Kiran saw Sheetal in tears. He didn't act since he didn't want to get in the way of her and Mom's chat.

"Sheetal, don't cry. How much you liked Theenal was known to us. Dear, don't hold yourself guilty.

Sheetal's father received the phone from Sheetal's mother.

"Hey there. You are a woman of resolve. We all live in harmony now that you have put in so much effort."

"Dad, I realise how much I hurt you."

"No matter how old you get, Sheetal, you will always be my little one. Nothing about anything is worth regretting. Additionally, we made mistakes as well and never made a serious effort to communicate with you."

"Mum and Dad, I love you both so much."

"We also love you a great deal. How are your travels going?

"It's quite pleasant. I'm now travelling to Mumbai by rail from Bangalore.

That's excellent. Are you by yourself?

"No, I got a travel companion from Munnar. An advocate named Kiran."

"Okay, dear, have fun on your travels."

"Goodbye, let's talk later."

The call got disconnected.

Kiran offered her a tissue.

When Sheetal received it, she apologised, saying, "I couldn't hide my emotions."

"Why are you apologising to me?" Kiran commented. You are no longer an alien, too. At last, you had shared your feelings. You did emerge from the box.

With a giggle, Sheetal replied, "You were right, they got extremely happy." Their smiles showed how happy they were. Even from here, I felt it.

Kiran answered, "It's called love." It's simple enough that you love your parents and they love each other.

Sheetal said, "Thanks, Kiran."

Kiran answered, "Never mind. Making you and your family happy made me incredibly joyful.

Sheetal grinned.

They ate lunch, listened to music, and watched films.

"I can't still figure out one thing," inquired Sheetal.

And Kiran said, "What?"

"Why did Jacob bro and Grace sis trust us so much, even though we were strangers?" Sheetal retorted.

"Some people can recognise who is good and who is bad," Kiran replied. They might have thought we were sincere since we were speaking the truth. Like we felt regarding Uncle Rafeek.

Sheetal answered, "Well, I see."

But never assume that everyone in this world is sincere, Kiran cautioned. Some people might not be good for us. They have to be talented actors.

Sheetal answered, "That is accurate. Similar to Grace Sis's family.

"Exactly," Kiran responded.

Kiran's expression went blank.

What happened suddenly? Sheetal asked.

Kiran glared at her and replied, "Nothin'. I was just thinking of someone.

"Kiara right," Sheetal remarked.

"Yes, no one has ever cheated me like her," Kiran remarked.

In response, Sheetal said, "Now what is she doing?"

"I had never stalked her after the breakup," Kiran retorted. My friend once informed me that she was employed by a company as a company secretary.

"We can talk about changing the topic or else you become gloomy," Sheetal remarked.

"Gloomy is the perfect synonym for Sheetal," Kiran remarked.

Sheetal erupted in laughter.

"Well, how does your bank work without the cashier?" Kiran inquired.

"The work is assigned to a co-worker," Sheetal retorted.

"Did you call your co-worker?" Kiran asked.

"For what?" inquired Sheetal.

Laughing, Kiran shot back, "He or she might need your guidance." Ultimately, you ought to be aware of how your bank is currently operating.

After giving it some thought, Sheetal found a vacant spot on the train and gave her co-worker Ganga a call.

"Hello. Who is this speaking for?"

"Hello, I am Sheetal."

It was unexpected, which is why Ganga was astonished.

"Any urgent business, ma'am?"

"No, if you have any questions about the job, don't hesitate to contact me or send me a message.

" Sure."

"Keep going."

"I'm grateful, ma'am."

Sheetal returned to Kiran. She gave a thumbs up.

They purchased drinks and snacks and ate them. They spend time watching movies and consuming supper.

They climbed to their separate berths during the night.

It was plenty cold because it was November.

Fortunately, they both had blankets.

They conveyed Goodnight and slept.

CHAPTER XX

MUMBAI

By 9 AM, they had arrived in Mumbai.

"Mumbai is more beautiful than in movies," said Kiran.

Indeed, it does, Sheetal retorted. What about our accommodation, too?

"My brother typically stays in a hotel close to Chhatrapati Shivaji when he travels to Mumbai for neurology sessions," Kiran remarked. He claimed that the rooms are decent and the costs are reasonable. We can travel there.

Sheetal said, "All right, let's head there."

They had breakfast from a stand selling street cuisine.

They arrived at the Hotel Plaza by bus.

They reserved rooms 102 and 103 for Kiran and Sheetal, two nearby rooms.

After going to their rooms, they had a bath. The long trip had left them sufficiently exhausted.

Just as Kiran was going to fall asleep, he heard someone knocking.

Kiran pulled open the door. Sheetal was the one.

"What's the matter?" he inquired.

"We need to talk," she said.

They sat down on the bed after Kiran greeted her.

"Well, my dad has a friend named Vasudev," Sheetal retorted. Ivory Crest Enterprises is the name of his construction company. I was once informed by my dad that a legal advisor position was vacant. I'm not sure if the vacancy is still open. I can give my father a call if that interests you.

Startled, Kiran retorted, "I'm intrigued. Give your dad a call."

Sheetal gave her father a call.

"Hey, Dad."

"Yes, tell her, dear."

"Dad, I just want to know if the legal advisor position at Vasudev's uncle's company is still open."

"I went jogging, and I met him." Despite the large number of applicants, he claimed that none had the necessary skills. For what purpose?"

"For my travel companion, Kiran."

"Alright. I'll give you Vasudev's phone number. And warmest wishes to him."

"Dad, thank you."

The call got disconnected.

"Dad said that it is still vacant," Sheetal retorted. This is the number of Vasudev's uncle. Give him a call.

Kiran gave him a call.

Kiran returned a few minutes later.

"What did he say", Sheetal enquired.

"He accepted for an online interview," Kiran retorted. He'll provide the time and link. We can wait for it.

On Kiran's phone, a notification appeared.

Kiran's gaze grew wide.

What occurred? Sheetal enquired.

Kiran said, "I have to join at 10:30," as he turned to face away. It is now 10:15 p.m. I'm not sure. I even own a fancy outfit.

"Don't you even have a formal shirt?" inquired Sheetal.

"I don't think so because it's a holiday trip, so I avoided formal shirts," Kiran retorted.

Sheetal answered, "It's possible. Save yourself the time. You check the necessary documents and share them with the soft copies after that. Please give your bag to me. I'll look around.

Kiran began to feel nervous. "I cannot allow a woman to go through my belongings."

"There is no time for your shyness, and we are running out of time," shouted Sheetal.

Sheetal grabbed his bag and started to search.

Kiran checked the time, 10:20, but he was helpless. He began sending Vasudev the necessary documentation.

Sheetal began searching for a formal shirt right away in his travel bag. She discovered fancy t-shirts, socks, and jeans, even his boxers.

Eventually, she noticed a single white formal shirt at the bottom of the suitcase.

Sheetal said, "YES I FOUND IT," with a sigh.

Kiran shot back, "WOW."

Sheetal looked at her watch; 10:24 a.m.

"Take this and get ready," Sheetal remarked.

Kiran opened his t-shirt to take it off. It flashed on him that Sheetal was present. With an uneasy smile, he hurried to the bathroom.

With a giggle, Sheetal set up the room. He returned.

He had on a zebra-striped pair of shorts and an elegant white shirt. She chuckled.

"It's all set", Sheetal declared. I had looked over the network. It's excellent.

Kiran answered, "I'm grateful. I feel a little anxious."

"There is no need for tension if you believe in yourself," Sheetal remarked. We are merely attempting. You can try your best, I'm sure. I'll be in my room.

Kiran gave a nod.

Sheetal entered her room.

Kiran joined the Google conference. Vasudev was already there at the conference.

"Good morning, sir."

"Good morning, Adv. Kiran Manohar, is that correct?"

"Yes, sir."

"Kiran, we don't conduct interviews conventionally, such as by posing standard questions. A formal, difficult interview is not what I desire. You are capable of sincere self-expression.

"Alright, sir."

"I've read your files. You top the university's rankings. Most people will write judicial exams or apply for jobs. How are you doing?"

"Sir, I was hoping to go to the Munsiff Magistrate Exam. Regretfully, a couple of events in my life prevented me from being able

to. In court, I worked as a junior advocate."

"Which types of cases you are dealing with?"

"Both civil and criminal. However, I specialise in civil cases."

"So tell me about any case in which you appeared in court."

"Sir, my client had approached me for a civil case. Their assets belonged to his dad alone. He passed away without dividing the estate. His father has two sons. My client was prepared to transfer all the assets to his brother. From his brother, he demanded a fair sum. The client's brother received a profitable offer. However, his brother wasn't prepared to contribute any cash or shares. The courtroom was the venue for the case. Our opponents were crafty. They even attempted to perpetrate fraud. But the triumph of our side was due to my communication, observational skills, and critical thinking. My client received more money than he had requested."

"Well, Mr. Kiran Manohar, I need to talk to our board about you. Ivory Crest Enterprises' policy is to notify you whether you are accepted or rejected along with the rationale behind your denial. It will help you to make better in your interviews."

"I'm grateful, sir."

The meeting came to an end.

Kiran let out a sigh and went to Sheetal's room.

Sheetal asked, "How was the interview?"

In response, Kiran said, "It was a little strange. I'm not sure. There are no expectations of me.

That's good, Sheetal said. I'm going hungry. Can we head over to lunch?

Kiran nodded.

After arriving at a hotel, they had lunch.

They returned to the Hotel Plaza.

Sheetal declared, "I'm so tired."

Kiran answered, "Me too."In the evening, we can go to destinations. Go now and have a nap.

They retired to their rooms, where they passed out.

Sheetal had a dream.

She was at a majestic palace in her dream. It was an enormous palace filled with exquisite artwork. There was a massive, sparkling golden chandelier.

She was astounded by the beauty.

Kiran was there too. A large number of people were clicking photos. Sheetal was giving the chandelier a deep look.

Abruptly, the joyful, vivid appearance transformed into a scary, pitch-black background. There was total quiet and no light. Her breath was audible to her. The occupants of the royal palace had vanished.

Her head had been struck by a white light beam. There was no other light like it. The light trailed after her.

Calling from Sheetal, "KIRAN, WHERE ARE YOU?"

Sheetal rushed to locate the exit door.

Sheetal failed to locate the door. She was anxious about Kiran.

At last, a ray of light caught her attention, and Kiran was standing there.

Sheetal raced.

She noticed that Kiran had a distinct look on her face. There was a divine shine, she thought, on his face. Instead of being tense, he was smiling.

Sheetal exclaimed, "What's going on here?"

With a smile, Kiran stated, "I just want to make something clear."

And Sheetal asked, "What?"

"I am just a piece of your thoughts," Kiran retorted.

Sheetal said, "I don't get it."

Kiran said, "Pay close attention. Sheetal, the loss of your sister has traumatised you, making you moody and depressed. Happiness was what your subconscious mind craved for. You produced me for your happiness."

Sheetal's eyes expanded and felt lightheaded.

"Kiran does exist only in your imagination, not in reality," Kiran went on.

Sheetal cried out, "Don't say that."

Kiran smiled and faded.

"Kiran, please don't leave me alone," cried Sheetal.

Sheetal awoke with a start. Her respiration was very rapid. She was sweating intensely.

She exclaimed, "What a nightmare!"

After taking a sip of water, she wondered, "What if it's a signal?"

She recalled the pictures. She shivered and unintentionally dropped her phone from her fingers as she reached for it to see the pictures.

She attempted to turn on the phone, but she was unable.

She ran to room 102 and rapped on the door.

"KIRAN OPEN THE DOOR!" was the cry she let out.

It flashed on her that the door was unlocked. After turning the knob, she stepped inside.

She was taken aback upon seeing the room. It was empty!

Kiran was gone, as was his backpack.

She felt devastated.

She took a seat on the bed.

She said, "It wasn't a dream! It was a wake-up call."

"Why, God, you're stealing my happiness," she sobbed again. You stole my sister, turned me into a rude person, and now you've made me mad. What sin do I commit to deserve these penalties?

She kept crying while covering her face.

"Hey, what happened to you, Sheetal?" asked Kiran leaning against the door.

"Oh, you return?" I am aware that you are not real," Sheetal answered.

"Did you consume something?" Kiran inquired. Why are you in tears?"

"Please don't make me vulnerable," Sheetal retorted. These are intolerable to me anymore. You are nothing more than a fantasy that I conjured up for my delight. I'm going to see a psychiatrist shortly.

"Madam, it looks like you had a nightmare," Kiran remarked. I am not a figment of your imagination.

Sheetal paused to reflect.

"Where did you go and why did you take your backpack?" she then inquired.

With a giggle, Kiran replied, "I went for a quick outing because I was bored." I went to your room after knocking twice on the door and finding you asleep. I also prefer to carry my backpack everywhere I go.

"I am still having hallucinations," Sheetal retorted.

In response, Kiran said, "I am a human being. Please make an effort to comprehend."

"NOO YOU AREN'T REAL!" exclaimed Sheetal. YOU ARE JUST THOUGHTS...

Kiran grew furious. With his hands resting on her shoulders, he let out a loud "SHEETAL!"

Kiran's unexpected behaviour caused Sheetal to become quiet and his face to turn scarlet.

Kiran retorted deeply looking her in the eyes, "Sheetal, I'm not your imagination, I'm not lying. You have experienced a bad dream just now."

He pulled out his phone and displayed the images.

"If I were your imagination, I wouldn't be in pictures," inquired Kiran.

Sheetal was glad. She was so happy that she even went insane. She embraced him tightly.

Kiran experienced a momentary surprise because he didn't anticipate this. Right then, he was not sure what to do.

Kiran gave her a gentle head pat.

When Sheetal entered her head, she became aware of what she had just done.

She put her hands away from him.

For a split second, they were embarrassed of themselves.

"Well, we can visit the carnival and do some street shopping too after 6 PM," Kiran said, breaking the ice.

Sheetal said, "All right. I'm heading to my room now.

After entering her room, Sheetal collapsed on her bed. When she considers the things she does, she feels ashamed. She felt awkward about hugging him.

They visited the grounds of the carnival.

Massive multicoloured lights were used to beautify the area. Many stores sell toys, bangles, earrings, and clothes, as well as rides like gigantic wheels and arcades.

The breathtaking magnificence of the carnival astounded the travel companions.

Kiran was deep in contemplation.

"What are you thinking?" inquired Sheetal.

"Could you please give me 500 rupees?" Kiran said.

"For what?" inquired Sheetal.

It's a secret, Kiran remarked.

Sheetal gave the money.

Kiran went to a store and purchased two tiny scissors, a small plastic cover, and a few white sheets. Kiran's behaviour perplexed Sheetal.

Kiran went up to a few underprivileged kids who were between the ages of 7 and 15. They were the street vendors' kids.

Kiran said, "Hey kids, can you help me cut these papers, then I will show a magic."

Kiran had rudimentary Hindi.

The older children showed no interest. They feared he would deceive them.

"Guys, I'm trustworthy." Please assist me in cutting these papers, Kiran pleaded.

Kiran eventually persuaded them.

The kids and our travel companions began tearing the papers into an empty area.

They eventually completed it.

Kiran took the plastic covers and put the torn paper pieces on them. He distributed these covers to the children.

"Why are you giving this to us, Uncle?" They inquired.

"We're all heading to the giant wheel. This is my magic," Kiran said.

Joy filled the kids.

"Consult your parents beforehand. "I'll wait right here," Kiran said.

To get their approval, the kids ran to their parents.

With a smile, Sheetal remarked, "I assume this is the surprise? However, I fail to see the purpose of these studies.

Kiran answered, "Let's see what happens."

The kids returned.

They said, "Uncle, they gave permission."

"Hey guys, hurry up. And when you're up high, throw those papers."

Kids gave a nod.

Kiran, Sheetal, and the kids visited the giant wheel operator.

The operator felt surprised.

The kids got on the giant wheel after Kiran offered them money.

Kiran urged Sheetal to hurry up.

"You guys enjoy," Sheetal retorted.

To which Kiran replied, "Come on, it has to be fun."

They went into the giant wheel as well.

The giant wheel started turning.

The kids were having fun on the ride. Kiran replied, "Come on, we have to have fun."

They also went into the giant wheel.

The small white papers had a pleasant impact as they dropped to the ground. Those on the ground smiled at this simple act. The children's innocent expressions reflected their excitement.

Sheetal glared at Kiran. He was taking in the sights of smiling smiles and the journey. It was hard for her to look away from him. The giant wheel had come to a standstill.

"Did you enjoy the ride?" Kiran inquired.

Sheetal was deep in contemplation.

Are you lost, Sheetal? Kiran enquired. How did the ride go?

Sheetal answered, "It was fabulous."

They stepped off the enormous wheel.

The kids came over to them, beaming with happiness.

A child said, "Uncle, thank you so much for this."

"All the credit goes to this, aunt," Kiran retorted. She had funded this.

A little lad walked up to her and motioned for her to go on her knees.

She bowed.

"Aunty, I never forget this day," he remarked. You're a good person.

Sheetal was pleased.

The kids said their goodbyes and left.

"They are also children, but because of their economic situation, they rarely got a chance to enjoy their childhood," Kiran retorted.

Sheetal said, "I gave you 500 rupees. You return me the priceless smiles of these kids."

"Wow, this is what I want to prove to you," Kiran remarked, clapping.

In response, Sheetal said, "Your surprise is great."

Kiran grinned and gave himself a happy rub on the back of his head.

Sheetal now saw the looks on his face.

In response, Kiran said, "Well, may we go shopping? I wish to purchase a few things.

"Of course," Sheetal remarked.

"I like the spirit now you possess," Kiran retorted.

For a moment, Sheetal got goosebumps.

They visited a clothing shop.

Kiran bought a traditional men's Kurta.

Sheetal's gaze settled on a ladies' segment of sky blue kurta with a white pattern.

Although Sheetal didn't generally like traditional clothing, she had an overwhelming desire to buy it. Along with a white palazzo, she bought it.

"I'm going to buy my parents a few clothes," Kiran declared.

Sheetal comprehended his suggestion to purchase clothing for her parents. She also bought them clothes.

After finishing their purchase at the clothing store, Kiran and Sheetal left.

Sheetal paused as they passed.

"What made you stop here?" Kiran enquired.

"I wish to buy a jhumka," Sheetal commented.

Are you serious? Kiran questioned.

In response, Sheetal said, "I'm going to buy it."

"Alright," Kiran replied.

She went with a white-patterned jhumka.

Sheetal put on a Jhumka and took off her black stud earrings.

Sheetal inquired, "How is this?"

Kiran commented, "Not good."

Sheetal frowned.

Kiran answered, "It was a lie. It suits you well.

Sheetal bought it.

They consumed street food.

They arrived at the hotel by hiring a rickshaw.

They retired to their rooms for a nap.

CHAPTER XXI

DO YOU LIKE FLYING

"Sheetal, open the door. It is ten in the morning. Kiran stated that we must have breakfast.

Sheetal opened the door as she awoke.

Sheetal indicated that she would be there in five minutes.

"All right, I'll wait in my room," Kiran replied.

After brushing her teeth, Sheetal returned.

Kiran answered, "Can we leave?"

Sheetal nodded.

They dined at a restaurant close to the Plaza Hotel.

"Do you like to fly?" Kiran questioned as they were eating.

Sheetal gave a huh-move.

Kiran asked the same question again.

Who else despises flying, Sheetal retorted. However, we are only human.

"There is an adventure activity called skydiving," Kiran remarked.

Sheetal acknowledged this. Are you going to jump off of a plane?

Kiran replied, "Yes, but not only me, we are going for that."

Sheetal asked, "Are you sure?"

Kiran said, "Mumbai, there is a company specialised in skydiving. If you are willing, we can go."

Sheetal asked. "It must be very expensive."

"Yes, but I will manage it. We are going for that," Kiran retorted.

"Are you sure?" Sheetal enquired

There is a company that specialises in skydiving in Mumbai," Kiran remarked. Let's go if you're willing.

Sheetal enquired. "It has to be costly."

"Yes, you are correct, but we will receive a 50% discount," Kiran said.

"The owner of that company is your relative, right?" mocked Sheetal.

"He was my client," Kiran remarked with a grin. The court verdict was favourable for him. He had guaranteed me that he would give me a reduced price. He is quite grateful to me.

Sheetal said, "I can't because that's only for you."

Kiran promised to persuade him. He might provide a discount.

"What was his case?" inquired Sheetal.

"Five of his customers got injured after skydiving," Kiran retorted.

Startled, Sheetal cried out, "Are you stupid? You intend to murder me.

Kiran chuckled out loud.

The hotel guests gazed at them.

Kiran expressed sorry for chuckling.

To which Kiran said, "It was a property case." I assisted him in receiving the money he was due. He was able to launch this business because of the money. Recently, he contacted me to let me know that his business is doing well and to offer me and the other person travelling with me a 50% discount. I was merely kidding about the injury of his customers."

"This guy," sighed Sheetal.

Softly spoken, Kiran said, "What happened, miss? Do you believe I'll push you into the hands of death?"

Admiring his voice, Sheetal forgot to respond.

"Hey," Kiran inquired.

Sheetal retorted, "I'm not sure." Please permit me to finish my meal.

"Well, we can start for Mumbai visiting after 2 PM," Kiran remarked. Because Mumbai's nighttime scenery is breathtaking. Our destinations include the Taj Hotel, the Gateway of India, and Chhatrapati Shivaji.

Sheetal answered, "That's fantastic."

They returned to the hotel.

"Well, give me your phone number," Kiran inquired. I neglected to inquire about that.

Sheetal provided her phone number. Kiran gave me a call.

"You can watch films or you can sleep," Kiran remarked. But don't tell me I am a ghost after taking a nap, OK?"

Sheetal gave a big laugh.

"So know how to laugh out loud," Kiran remarked.

She said, "I am human," Sheetal.

With a wave, they each departed to their rooms.

After carefully trying to turn on her phone, Sheetal had managed to fix it. Fortunately, it was in good condition.

She looked through her Instagram pictures with Olivia, Jacob, Kiran, and Grace. She set the phone down and began to reflect on the events of the past few days.

"Kiran is a chatterbox and hard to handle, but he is special," she thought to herself.

She made an effort to push the idea away.

"Not especially notable; I simply overanalyzed."

She watched one movie and scrolled over social media for a while.

They returned to the hotel after eating lunch at the same restaurant.

"Get ready, and put on any traditional clothing you may have," Kiran said. Because the Gateway of India, where we are headed, is the ideal setting for spectacular photos.

Sheetal gave a nod.

A short while after, Kiran was dressed in a *red kurta* and *black pants* he bought yesterday.

In that outfit, he appeared more handsome.

He knocked on Sheetal's door.

"Just five minutes," she remarked.

As he was pulling his sleeves back, Sheetal pulled open the door.

Kiran gazed at her. For a moment, he was motionless.

She was dressed in a *sky-blue kurta with white embroidery* that she had purchased yesterday, along with a *white palazzo*. Additionally, her jhumka enhanced her beauty.

"Finally, you become a woman," Kiran retorted.

Sheetal chuckled, asking, "Do I look good? My hairstyle might not go well with this outfit.

"To be honest, your boy cut hairstyle and this attire blends," Kiran retorted.

With a laugh, Sheetal thanks.

"I never expected you in traditional dress," Kiran said.

"You also look stunning in this red kurta," Sheetal retorted.

Kiran answered, "I'm grateful. Can we begin our journey now?

"Yes," Sheetal replied.

They walked to the Mumbai Museum also known as Chhatrapati Shivaji Monument.

Once they had the ticket, they went into the museum.

Sheetal said, "The architecture was impressive."

"UNESCO acknowledged this museum as a World Heritage Site in 2018," Kiran remarked.

Sheetal replied, "Oh I see."

The three areas of the museum were designated for natural science, art, and archaeology.

Here, our travel companions had the opportunity to visit numerous galleries. They observed sculptures, statues of Buddha, and a plethora of other artwork.

They weren't even aware they spent that much time in the Mumbai Museum, so they left after two hours.

By bus, they arrived at the Gateway of India.

Across from the Gateway of India, they could see the Taj Hotel.

"If I become rich. I will stay at the Taj Hotel for a night or two," Kiran retorted.

Sheetal chuckled.

They visited the Gateway of India.

They observed a group of pigeons flying and consuming grains in the evening.

"Perfect Bollywood scene," exclaimed Sheetal.

"Yes," Kiran retorted, "but they could ruin your mood by putting a surprise on your dress." You still want to spend as much time as you can with them.

Sheetal remarked, "Yuck, let's move on."

They passed through the India Gateway.

Kiran took a single picture of Sheetal, and Sheetal took his picture.

With the assistance of an unknown person, they also shot a group photo.

"The pictures are nice, aren't they?" Kiran remarked.

"The Gateway of India is so beautiful," Sheetal retorted.

In response, Kiran said, "We are also gorgeous."

Kiran's phone rang all of a sudden.

It was Vasudev's call.

Vasudev, sir, is calling. Oh, my god. He'll reveal the outcome. "I'm anxious," Kiran said.

Sheetal motivated him, "Attend it."

Kiran was there.

"Hello, sir."

"Hi Kiran, I gave you a call to inform you of Ivory Crest Enterprises' decision."

"All right, sir."

"How will you respond if I tell you that you are rejected?"

"Sir, I will honour your decision and investigate the cause of your denial based on Ivory Crest Enterprises' suggestion. And give it another go."

"Unfortunately, you are ideal for this position."

Kiran was shocked.

"Greetings from Ivory Crest Enterprises, Kiran Manohar. You are appointed."

Joy filled Kiran's eyes.

"I'm very grateful, sir."

The call was disconnected.

Sheetal asked, "What did Kiran say?"

Kiran expressed his delight gently.

He embraced her and replied, "I don't know how to express my gratitude. I was worried about my life after this journey. I had searched for this company. The salary package is impressive. Thank you so much."

Sheetal was frozen until Kiran dropped the hug.

In response, Sheetal said, "I'm happy for you. Congratulations.

Kiran answered, "I'm grateful. All credit goes to this girl.

With a smile, Sheetal adored his fulfilment.

They set off on a boat ride.

The boat set out. They observed the sun's bright rays and soaring birds.

"This reminds me of our experience on the island," Sheetal remarked.

"Please don't remind me," Kiran said.

"Are you afraid of that too much?" inquired Sheetal.

"No, it was exciting to be trapped on an unknown island," Kiran shot back.

Sheetal chuckled.

"Well, my office is in Trivandrum," Kiran remarked.

"The Ivory Crest office is near my bank," Sheetal retorted.

"That's nice," remarked Kiran.

The boat set out on its return trip.

They watched as the boat moved, revealing bright lights.

"Kiran, notice how the location we previously saw has shifted. This is so beautiful!" remarked Sheetal.

That is accurate. "I can't believe my eyes," Kiran remarked.

Sheetal couldn't take her eyes off Kiran's face.

"The lovely ambience, striking lights, and his contentment.

His red kurta makes him more charming

He is childish and difficult to handle but he is special.

My eyes will never get bored by looking at those magnificent eyes.

If the time stuck now, I will be the most happiest person ever," she pondered.

Their eyes locked.

"Madam lost in your thoughts, the boat has stopped," Kiran replied with a smile. We must leave.

Sheetal emerged from her thoughts.

They saw the unique performance at the Gateway of India.

After eating dinner at a hotel, they returned to the Hotel Plaza.

After saying goodbye, they retired to their rooms.

Sheetal pondered over every episode involving Kiran.

Her thoughts were:-

In the beginning, he was annoying. I disliked him. But he held the key to my contentment.

The beam of illumination that drove away the dark clouds from my existence.

I began to admire highly of him. I want him to be with me eternally after my dream.

Yes, I am falling in love with him.

However, how will I confess it?

Will a woman like me win his heart?

In any case, I can't suppress my feelings. Even if it hurts, I will accept his rejection.

She decided to express to him that she loves him tomorrow. She had slept soundly.

CHAPTER XXII

REALISATION

Sheetal knocked on door of room no. 102.

"Good morning, come in," Kiran said as she answered the door.

Sheetal went into the bedroom.

"We can go eat breakfast," Kiran suggested. We can then schedule our day after.

Sheetal answered, "Lead the way."

They entered the restaurant, ordered the food, and started eating.

Kiran said, "Sheetal, we have to go to the skydiving company today to collect the information."

Sheetal gave a nod.

After finishing their breakfast, they reached the skydiving company. They met the owner of the company. Dinesh was his name.

It cheered him to meet Kiran. He consented to provide Kiran and Sheetal with a discount.

They took a lesson that served as a guide for a skydiving trip and signed a few papers.

Tomorrow was supposed to be their dive day. They should wear tight clothing tomorrow, the trainer advised them.

At eleven a.m., they departed the company.

"Are you hungry?" Kiran said as they walked by.

Sheetal said in response, "Not that much."

In response, Kiran said, "How about going to a park?"

Sheetal declared she was ready.

They moved in the direction of a park with an abundance of trees.

"Perfect place for getting fresh air," said Kiran.

They walked across the velvety emerald lawns. He paused and studied the sky for a moment.

Sheetal made a 'what' gesture.

"Wait," Kiran said.

He picked up a book and a blue mat with white patterns on it.

"Sheetal, I'm going to lie down because it will be a good experience to lie down and breathe the fresh air," Kiran stated, placing the mat on the ground. Additionally, the sun is not as intense.

He handed the book to Sheetal, who was sitting on the mat.

Kiran said, "Avoid using the phone currently. It will ruin this moment. Go through this book"

"All right, may I lie down?" Sheetal asked.

Kiran said, "Why not? I purchased this mat for my travel companion. He was unable to attend the picnic that we had scheduled.

Sheetal enquired, "Anyway, thanks. I'm happy to accompany you on your journey.

With a smile, Kiran replied, "You're welcome."

After setting the book on the ground, Sheetal took a seat close to Kiran.

Sheetal picked up the book to read.

They appreciated the serene aura of the park.

When Sheetal peeked at Kiran ten minutes later; he was fast asleep.

Sheetal considered,

"The loquacious, impulsive, hyperactive advocate became a calm, tranquil, and relaxed man. I have never seen somebody have the kind of charm that this man has in my entire life.

Though it could be awkward if he opened his eyes, she couldn't take her eyes off of him. She read the book through again.

Kiran opened his eyes and stood up after an hour.

"I apologise. I accidentally took a nap." he yawned in a sleepy tone.

Sheetal fixed his messy hair and offered an encouraging word.

They head to a local restaurant as they leave the park.

In the local restaurant:-

"I am sure we are going to experience something new tomorrow," Kiran retorted.

That is accurate, Sheetal stated. I was a little anxious, but I feel better after attending the basic class.

There's no reason to worry, Kiran said. Alright, the day after tomorrow we can go back to Kerala. I intend to get a flight ticket.

Sheetal concurred.

They made reservations for flights from Mumbai to Trivandrum.

They had to wait for their order.

"It will be a perfect time to confess my feelings to him," Sheetal thought to herself.

Sheetal inhaled deeply.

Kiran caught sight of it.

Sheetal uttered, "Kiran, I would like to-."

A woman suddenly walked up to Kiran

When he saw her, he was shocked, and Sheetal was perplexed.

The woman's actions demonstrated her boastfulness and guile.

Kiran got out of the chair.

The woman ran to hug him.

Sheetal's angry eyes mirrored Kiran's expressionless rage.

The woman remarked,"What a delightful surprise, Kiran! I never imagined we would cross paths again. The destiny is indeed genuine. I was with my colleagues on a tour.We even had plans to go to another restaurant, but we ended up coming here."

"Sheetal, this is Kiara," Kiran introduced.

For a moment, Sheetal thought that time had stopped. She put on a false smile to mask her emotions.

Unpleasantly, Kiara enquired, "Kiran, who is this lady? Tour guide?"

"No, she is my travel companion," Kiran retorted.

"Never mind," Kiara said, with a wicked smile and a pitying expression.

Sheetal didn't like how Kiara approached Kiran or her behaviour.

"Come on, Kiran, we need to talk," Kiara said with an artificially pleasant tone as she grabbed Kiran's right wrist.

With a pitying look, Kiara said to Sheetal, "Excuse me, you stay here." We would like to speak.

Kiara forced him out of the restaurant with force.

Helplessly, Sheetal watched the incident unfold.

Sheetal lost herself in thought:-

Why does she approach him and I feel bad?

What if she succeeds in winning him?

She is much better than me.

Who else loves a mundane and rude female like me?

A jumble of thoughts strayed into her consciousness.

Kiran arrived and took a seat in the chair after a short while.

When Kiara dragged him away. His face was blank and bewildered; now, he was beaming.

With a smile on her face, Sheetal enquired, "What you guys talked about for so long?"

"She told me that I was the perfect boyfriend for her," a shy Kiran added. She had dated a few guys before realising my worth. She asked whether I would be interested in getting back together and marry her.

Sheetal felt her heart throbbing so badly.

Falsely grinning, she enquired, "What you said?"

"I said that I will give a reply soon," Kiran remarked with a gentle smile.

With a faint smile, Sheetal asked, "Do you love her?"

"Yes, I am glad she has returned to my life," Kiran answered.

"What if she makes the same mistake again?" Sheetal questioned.

Kiran met Sheetal's eyes directly. Sheetal struggled to keep eye contact.

With his eyes fixed on hers, Kiran proclaimed, "There is a quote,

"'If you truly love someone and if they leave, you wait for them.

If they come back, it's for you.'"

This quote is true, right? Is this quote accurate?"

For her, it was a thunderclap. Her final hope is gradually vanishing from her existence.

Sheetal retorted, "I'm not sure."

"Whenever I see her. I forget all of my pain and sorrows," Kiran replied. It brings me joy to be around here. However, I'm confused.

"Kiran, if you love her truly and she loves the ways of you do, then confess it or else you may lose her," Sheetal stated with a sincere smile.

Kiran answered, "You're right."

Sheetal asked whether she could go to the hotel.

"What happened?" Kiran enquired.

"Headache, I just want to sleep," Sheetal retorted. You go hang out with her. Spend time with those you love deeply.

"That's correct, but how do you go alone?" Kiran inquired.

"I'm not a kid," Sheetal declared with a smile. I'm going to hire an autorickshaw.Kiran, have fun with your time

After eating to the end, they made the required payment.

After saying their goodbyes, Kiran and Sheetal parted ways.

It was the first time they came across two distinct locations.

After arriving at the Hotel Plaza, Sheetal quickly went to her room. She went in and shut the door.

She sobbed as she sat on her bed.

Sheetal vented her emotions to the room's walls.

She sobbed for a few minutes before washing her face in the bathroom. She turned to face herself in the vanity mirror.

She used a towel to clean her face.

She spoke while smiling.

Why are you crying like a child, Sheetal? I understand that accepting Kiran is not mine may be difficult for me. He deserves happiness because he is a wonderful man. Kiran loves Kiara because she will be a good person. I might have misjudged her.

Kiran is deeply embedded in the depths of my heart unknowingly. He only takes a few days to win over your heart. I fell in love with him and I never fell in love again other than him.

I assure you that I had abandoned my past nasty self. She will never come back.

There are many individuals in this world, and I plan to spend my entire life helping and socialising with them. I will always remember the things I learned from my sunshine.

I will gladly encourage their marriage. Even their names match Kiran and Kiara. It is the victory of Kiran's love. I will leave his life after the completion of this journey.

It must hurt, but either I will have to live with this wound or it will heal. A lovely wound."

Grinning widely, she glanced at her mirror.

At last, she realised how she might bring her happiness. Kiran taught it.

At night, Kiran came back. He brought a food parcel for Sheetal. He handed it on to her.

Sheetal observed a glow and contentment on his face.

He's happy without me, she thought to herself. No matter how much we love someone, we cannot force them to love us.

She smiled at Kiran, too.

Kiran inquired, "What makes you smile?"

"I was excited about skydiving," said Sheetal, in deceit.

"I assure you never forget it," Kiran retorted.

Sheetal grinned.

"Sheetal, I'm considering staying longer on vacation. Can my airline tickets be cancelled? Kiran inquired, "Are you okay with travelling alone?"

"I don't mind travelling alone because I had intended to go on a solo trip. Sheetal shot back, "You can cancel it and spend time with her."

Kiran grinned shyly.

"Thanks for the food," Sheetal remarked with a smile as she fixed her gaze on him. I will Google pay for the cost of the package, the plane ticket, and any other costs."

All right," Kiran replied.

The phone rang for Kiran.

Kiran blushed upon noticing the call.

Good night, and let me take this call," Kiran murmured.

With a smile, Sheetal said, "Good night."

Sheetal slept with a lot of repressed feelings.

CHAPTER XXIII

SKY DIVING

Sheetal gave Kiran a call.

"Hello, Kiran."

"Yes, tell Sheetal."

"Could you be ready half an hour ahead of the scheduled time?"

"What took place?"

"Not anything significant."

"All right, I'll get ready in ten minutes."

Sheetal was waiting for him in front of room number 102 after ten minutes.

Asking, "Why did you tell me to get ready early?" Kiran opened the door.

"Well, can we go for a walk?" asked Sheetal.

Kiran concurred.

Following the instructor's advice, they were dressed in gym outfits.

The soft morning light and the sound of the birds chirping created a tranquil mood.

They observed a few people who came to jog.

While walking, Kiran inquired, "Why did you call me for a walk? Typically, you don't, that's why I asked."

"I usually exercise to maintain a healthy body," Sheetal stated. However, I put it on hold for this trip.

Kiran answered, "I don't get it?"

"I called you for a walk because today will be the last day of our journey," Sheetal retorted.

"Oh, I see," Kiran replied. How fast the days had passed. I shall always remember our journey.

"We will separate after skydiving," Sheetal retorted.

Kiran gave a nod.

Sheetal said, "Thanks for everything," as she looked directly into his eyes. I might not have known authentic happiness if you hadn't entered my life. I know I've caused you a lot of trouble. Please pardon me.

"No need to apologise," Kiran retorted.

Sheetal commented with a smile, "Don't change your bubbly character for anyone. I am sure Kiara will always love you."

"I never change my character don't worry," Kiran replied.

"That's all we can go to the skydiving centre," Sheetal retorted.

They arrived at the office after hiring an autorickshaw.

They arrived at the skydiving firm.

A few individuals were observed leaping from the sky and landing safely on the earth. After seeing them, they get additional guts.

They noticed someone correctly tying parachutes as soon as they walked into the workplace.

They noticed Dinesh coming their way.

"Hello, travel companions. The formalities are all finished. Have any of you had breakfast yet?

"No," they replied.

"You should eat before the dive or else you may feel tired," Dinesh said. The cafeteria is located there, so go and eat.

They purchased two sandwiches and two teas from the cafeteria. And consumed it.

"How was the food?" Dinesh inquired as they returned.

They gave thumbs up.

A staff said, "You are requested to be seated here. The instructors are busy while handling a few batches.

They gave a nod.

They watch an animated video on television that explains the rules of skydiving.

Kiran's phone rang

"I'll be back in a few minutes," Kiran said.

Sheetal gave a nod.

She thought:-

"I'm proficient at acting appropriately. The irony is that he will never know the intensity of my love."

Sheetal considered jumping as a way to get over her setback.

Kiran returned.

"Sir and Madam please keep your belongings in the cloakroom," a staff member remarked as they walked up. Cameras and phones are not allowed. We'll film your dive.

Their belongings are stored in the cloakroom.

"You are requested to use the washroom as it may be difficult for you to use it after wearing the harness," the employee added as she approached.

They each headed to the loo.

They met with the instructors after returning.

They were brought to the area designated for the fittings.

Our travel companions packed their harnesses with the help of the employees.

They were photographed by a staff.

"You guys are looking so cute," he said.

For a moment, Kiran and Sheetal gazed at one another.

"Don't touch or try to change your harness," the instructor said. It could cause a serious injury.

They became terrified.

Don't worry, the instructor added with a smile, "My name is Johnny. I am Sheetal Mam's instructor.

"And Tarun is my name. Kiran sir has me as his instructor, sir.

They said hello to them.

They had to ride in a vehicle to get to the sport, so they left the building.

After a few minutes, they arrived at the location.

Alongside the employees, they boarded the aircraft.

"Kiran, are you nervous?" asked Sheetal.

"A bit." Anyhow, I am aware of your anxiety. "Let us relish this," Kiran said.

The procedure for the skydiving was that the plane would land at a specific location, and our travel companions would jump alongside their respective instructors.

The aircraft had come to a stop.

Sheetal and Kiran sent their warmest wishes your way.

At first, Kiran and Tarun dived in.

In a matter of minutes, Johnny and Sheetal had jumped.

Our travel companions had the same experience.

They both had an extraordinary experience.

At first, anxiety and stress. They began to appreciate the moment after realising that their level of terror had subsided after a short while. In addition to being competent, the instructors encouraged their customers to enjoy their dives.

The divers conveyed their delight on camera adequately while filming the dives of Kiran and Sheetal.

They believed they had wings.

It is impossible to explain this feeling through words.

A moment with paradise.

They even desired to live forever in the sky and fly like birds.

The instructors opened the parachutes.

Among the most memorable events of their thirty years of existence, this one stood out.

Tarun and Kiran touched down first.

Sheetal and Johnny touched down a short while after.

She was still thrilled with anticipation.

Her eyes were searching for him.

Abruptly, she recognised a familiar voice, "SHEETAL".

She turned around.

She was astonished to see the few men in a U-shape, some holding plates with rose petals, while others were holding violins guitars, drums and a flute. Tarun, Johnny, and Dinesh were also there.

Kiran was coming towards her in the midst.

Sheetal became perplexed. "Kiran, is this applause for successfully finishing the skydiving?"

The group of people laughed.

Kiran indicated that was incorrect with a nod.

Puzzled Sheetal spotted something.

Something was in Kiran's right hand, but he hid.

"What's in your right hand?" asked Sheetal.

Kiran kneeled to the ground and raised his head.

He took out the bright red rose bouquet.

Raising his right hand, he presented the bouquet.

Sheetal had a rapid heartbeat.

Cheering broadly, Kiran held the bouquet while gazing lovingly into her stunning eyes.

With a sincere and gentle asking, he said, "*Sheetal, you are my travel companion. Will you be my life companion?*"

Tears filled her eyes, yet she was also confused, as he asked sincerely and gently, "Sheetal, you are my travel companion. Will you be my life companion?"

"Yes," Sheetal answered, "but what about Kiara?"

"I will tell this if you take this bouquet," Kiran remarked.

With a smile, Sheetal accepted the bouquet.

Sheetal offered her hand, and Kiran stood up from the ground.

Kiran began to describe the specifics of what had occurred yesterday.

When Kiara returned, he was taken aback.

Additionally, Kiran failed to escape her hug because he never expected one. When Kiara disrespected Sheetal, he became outraged.

He stepped outside to find out what she was planning when she grabbed him out of the restaurant.

Kiara said in an attractive tone, "I dragged you out of the restaurant since there's no privacy to spend our moments."

"What do you mean by 'our moments'?" Kiran asked

"Well, let me tell you this. Throughout our time in college, I knew you loved me unconditionally. Additionally, you had anguish when we split up. Anyway, things are going well now. With a fictitious cheerful voice, Kiara said, "I had relationships after our relationship, but none of the boys loved me like you did."

Kiran asked, "What exactly do you want?" and his expression made it clear he was not interested in talking to her."

I chatted with a couple of your pals. I'm aware that you're not dating right now. And if you will allow me the opportunity to make amends, I know you genuinely love me. We might, after all, begin dating and get married.

"I am feeling so sorry that God forgot to give you an emotion called shame," Kiran replied, laughing out loud.

"You are being so rude," Kiara said, becoming agitated.

Kiran answered, "Am I being rude? You know what you have done throughout my life. And boldly making me a proposal, correct?"

"For me, our relationship was not serious," Kiara yelled back. If you think of it as a serious relationship, I won't be held responsible.

"DID YOU EVER SAY, IT WASN'T A SERIOUS RELATIONSHIP?" shouted Kiran.

Kiara was at a loss for words to respond.

Kiran answered, "I know you can't answer that question," with a smile. All you did was pretend to love me to obtain the things you wished. You're tired of disloyal guys who are exactly like you. All you need is a loyal husband. You didn't even harbour any guilt, I'm sure of it. Until you love someone genuinely, you will never be able to comprehend my pain."

Kiara played the innocent part, swallowing her rage, and added, "Kiran, there is a quote:

> *'If you truly love someone and if they leave, you wait for them.*
>
> *If they come back, it's for you.'*

I am yours. Please give me a second chance."

"Nice quote, but you can't heal the wound that you made a few years ago," he smirked and remarked.

> *" If we truly love someone and*

If they love us the same,
They will stay with us even though the situations distance us.
That's love."

Go from my life, please.

Kiara began to cry artificially.

"Your tears have been concealed with the fakeness of your mind," Kiran remarked. Do you even feel guilty about stalking me around?

Kiara wiped away her tears, realising her plan had not worked.

Kiara was ready to go.

"And for your kind information, the woman sitting next to me is not my tour guide," Kiran stated. She is my love. The woman who opened the chambers of my heart, which were closed due to an evil woman for a few years. I will propose to her tomorrow."

"What if she rejects you?" inquired Kiara.

With a smile, Kiran declared, *"It won't ever make me stop loving her."* She is the only person I have a place for in my heart. I shall bear her rejection, even though it hurts. Furthermore, please don't ever return to my life. Be a decent person even if you don't have much goodness.

Kiara flashed him an introspective look before leaving.

Kiran concluded her explanation of the enigma to Sheetal.

"Then what about phone calls and where were you yesterday evening?" inquired Sheetal.

"It was Dinesh, sir," Kiran remarked, fixing his gaze on Dinesh. I was talking to him about the proposal plan for today. And I was here for the arrangements in the evening. To give you a surprise, I decided to hide these.

Kiran went on, "The mystery has been resolved. I'm asking the same question again now.

YOU ARE MY TRAVEL COMPANION, WILL YOU BE MY LIFE COMPANION."

Sheetal's eyes lit up with happiness and fulfilment.

"YES DEAR", she said, I feared that I would lose you.

The petals were thrown by the employees.

The rose petals and the sound of the instruments enhanced the beauty of the moment.

Kiran grinned broadly, delighted. He gave her a forehead kiss while closing his eyes.

With blushing, Sheetal rose to plant a kiss on his left cheek.

"The same cheek you slapped," Kiran replied while laughing.

"I knew it," Sheetal remarked.

Tears welled up in their eyes with smiles.

They embraced tightly.

They were over the moon.

They had their eyes closed because they were experiencing the most exquisite feeling —love.

The beauty of their love was praised by those in attendance. They joyfully clapped with their hands.

Dinesh walked up to him and said, "Match made in heaven."

They were lost in the moment, so they didn't hear that. The group laughed together.

Dinesh gave me a "Hello."

They broke up their hug

"Match made in heaven," Dinesh said once more.

They flushed.

Dinesh remarked, "Kiran is the genius behind this, Sheetal. All I did was encourage him. Because of his talkative demeanour, you may assume he is not very intellectual, but in reality, he is a sharp-minded individual. His intelligence helped me get funding and launch my business."

"Oh, I see," Sheetal remarked.

Kiran was beaming.

Dinesh retorted, "Sheetal is a gem, Kiran. I can read it from her eyes. She adores you tremendously. Keep her close at hand".

Gazing at her, Kiran said, "Yes, without a doubt."

"I'm glad to see you guys together," Dinesh went on. Since I constantly think of my wife whenever I watch a love illustration, I always support true love.

They chuckled.

"She is sweet, but her anger is horrible," Dinesh remarked.

Everyone started laughing.

They said goodbye to Dinesh and the company employees and retrieved their bags from the cloakroom.

They got onto a bus. In the seats, they sat.

While riding the bus, "How was the experience?" asked Kiran.

"I was speechless. I never thought you loved me back as I do," Sheetal replied.

Kiran chuckled and remarked, "I was sceptical about you. I have no idea how you would respond, even if I proposed to you.

Nevertheless, I decided to ask you out regardless of whether you say yes or no."

"I appreciate your courage," Sheetal remarked.

With a blush on his cheeks, Kiran said, "Thanks."

"Next up is our bust stop," stated Sheetal.

After getting off the bus, they went to the Hotel Plaza.

They prepared to go to the airport by packing their belongings.

They spent a minute exploring rooms 102 and 103. These walls were aware of their emotions before they were.

Kiran said, "I don't know why I am feeling something special about room no. 102 and 103, especially 102."

"Because they knew our love before we discovered it," Sheetal grinned.

Startled, Kiran retorted, "You sound like a poet."

"But not good like you," Sheetal remarked. I believe there is a secret writer inside of you. You ought to write novels."

After pausing to think, Kiran said, "I will try."

They exited the Hotel Plaza and reached Mumbai Airport through a taxi.

After completing the procedures, they went inside the plane and seated on their seats.

CHAPTER XXIV

MUMBAI TO TRIVANDRUM

Kiran was seated beside Sheetal in the window seat of the plane.

The air hostess served the lunch to them.

Since they had skipped lunch, they happily ate it. They completely forgot about it.

"How long will it take us to reach Trivandrum?" Sheetal inquired.

"Two hours and thirty minutes," Kiran said.

Sheetal said, "Okay, by the way, how will you go to Kollam?"

Kiran remarked, "Keerthan and Nihal will pick me.

"Your brother is Keerthan. Nihal, who is he?" asked Sheetal.

Keerthan's best friend is Nihal, Kiran remarked with a smile. Since elementary school, they have been close friends. Nihal works as an interior designer. They manage to get together at least once a month despite their hectic schedules.

Sheetal remarked, "That's nice."

"Nihal frequently visits our home," Kiran remarked. To us, he is like a family member. But these pleasant individuals troubled me.

They chuckled.

"But they are coming to pick you up in the evening," Sheetal remarked.

Puzzled, Kiran remarked, "I still can't figure out what their intention is behind this."

What occurred, Sheetal enquired.

Kiran answered, "Keerthan called me today, and we had a nice conversation. He had asked me about my trip back. He willingly agreed to come to fetch me with Nihal. They constantly strive to cause trouble. They are helping me for the first time.

Sheetal advised against his over-analyzing.

Guys, Kiran was right to be sceptical.

A few hours prior, at Kiran's residence.

Since Keerthan had taken a leave and Nihal was available, Nihal visited Keerthan.

Nihal sensed that Keerthan was not quite right.

Nihal asked, "Buddy, why are you looking so different?"

"I'm perplexed," Keerthan uttered.

"Who is it that puzzles you? It must be your girlfriend, Nihal teasingly said.

With a furious expression on his face, Keerthan cried out, "You know I don't have a girlfriend, so why are you making fun of me? I will strike you if you do this again.

From the kitchen, yelled his mother, "Stop acting like kids."

Nihal laughed and said, "A handsome young neurologist, but talking like a sensitive kid."

Keerthan forced his rage to simmer.

You know my brother went on a trip, Nihal? Keerthan said, "I think he got a girlfriend."

"I find it hard to believe that," said Nihal

"Look, I believe they are dating," Keerthan remarked, displaying a photo of the two of them taken at Munnar.

Nihal questioned, "Did you ask your brother about this?"

'Yes', he informed Keerthan that she was his travel companion.

Then, he is correct. Nihal said, "You are the one telling stories."

Keerthan questioned, "Why are you saying like this?"

"You once said that Kiran Bro's hidden lover was the woman in a picture that you showed to me. Later on, we learned that was incorrect. She thought of your brother as her sibling. It was your brother who persuaded her and her lover's family through conversation. We attend their wedding. Keep me out of this," said Nihal.

"You were the one who was eager to call that girl and inquire about this, and you shared my opinion. Now you are acting like an innocent, yelled Keerthan.

"Calm down. Nobody would like you if you rant like this, Nihal declared.

"I have a lot of fans right now, so it's not a big deal, right?" Keerthan asked sarcastically.

"You have a lot of fans. Nihal remarked, "I don't even understand why you are still single despite your attractive appearance and charming demeanour.

"Don't make me feel good. All I want is for my brother to get married. Then, Keerthan remarked, only I could get married.

"Your brother is a strange person. Due to a breakup that occurred during his time at college, he is still unmarried. Unlike your brother, people will get back together right away after a split, Nihal observed.

"She wasn't serious, but he did truly love her." This continued for the entire five years of their relationship. I like arranged marriage because of this, Keerthan said.

That is depressing. However, he needs to go on. If not, don't worry; you will follow in the footsteps of great unmarried people, Nihal mocked.

"Shut up. I'm disturbed that even you are engaged. Keerthan remarked, "I am happy about you, but still, I can't imagine that."

"Don't worry, all is well," Nihal remarked.

Keerthan came into Kiran's story while browsing Instagram.

When Keerthan opened it, he said, "WOWWWWWWW.

Nihal gasped. "What takes place? Did you receive a rise in salary?"

Keerthan jumped out of the chair and performed a little dance.

Nihal said, "Are you alright? Why are you acting in this manner?

As Keerthan said, "The wait is over. My greatest hope had materialised. God, I am grateful.

Nihal was fed up with Keerthan.

"I might break your bones if you continue this drama," yelled Nihal.

For a moment, Keerthan's cheerful expression faded.

He revealed Nihal the Instagram story of Nihal.

Nihal exclaimed, "Unbelievable."

It was the photo captured by the skydiving company's staff. Kiran and Sheetal were hugging in the photo.

"Yeah, my assumption was correct," Keerthan exclaimed.

Nihal muttered, "Lower your volume or else Aunty will hit us."

"I'll tell Mom about this," Keerthan added.

"No, that is not within our authority to say. Nihal remarked, "Kiran bro will tell about her."

"I'll ask my brother about this over the phone," Keerthan added.

"Remain calm, my friend. Avoid ruining the fun. Tell me when he's arriving, Nihal replied, and we can go pick him up from Trivandrum.

With a smile on their faces, Keerthan and Nihal said, "Yeah, we're going to meet our sister-in-law."

During the flight,

"Kiran, may I ask you a question?" Sheetal asked.

"Sure," Kiran answered.

"When did you start to love me?" asked Sheetal

"Nice question," Kiran remarked, grinning. Well, in the beginning, I just wanted you to be my travel companion because I hated to travel alone. However, I felt that we couldn't become travel companions after witnessing your impolite behaviour, so I considered going alone. After we got acquainted with Olivia and the Christian couple, you gradually began to alter.

"Grace sis made me realise my mistakes, then?', said Sheetal.

"I was impressed by your calmness when we were trapped on the island, remarked Kiran.

Actually? Sheetal chuckled, "You fall for my calmness."

"It may sound odd. But the calmness and optimistic quality you showed fascinated me. And we shared about our lives. And I don't even know how I slowly fall in love with you. I met a lot of women but you were special," said Kiran.

His cheeks were blushing.

"You're blushing, haha," Sheetal remarked.

It's quite typical. And you realised something when you gave me a hug following your dreadful dream? "I missed one of my heartbeats," Kiran remarked.

Sheetal's eyes expanded. "Really?"

Kiran remarked, "I don't know how to describe my situation at that time."

"All right, I didn't do it on purpose. That awful dream really disturbed me, and when I realised you weren't a hallucination, it was a blissful moment for me.," Sheetal said.

"I saw your vulnerable side the moment you embraced me. I saw that you were trying to hide your weak side by acting rudely and haughtily. You were entitled to happiness. And I promised," Kiran retorted, giving her a mild glare.

"What was the assurance?" inquired Sheetal.

After giving her eyes a serious look, Kiran said, *"I will protect this woman and keep her happy."*

"I don't have words to say, Mr. Kiran," Sheetal grinned.

"Who is blushing now?" Kiran teasingly said.

"I understand it's natural. Proceed," Sheetal chuckled.

"Oh, I see," Sheetal remarked.

"I am still ecstatic that you feel the same way about me," Kiran remarked.

"Well, when I started my journey, I saw a dream. I found myself lost in an unidentified, pitch-black place. I ran through the tunnel in an attempt to get away from the location. I finally came across a light after running for so long. I dreamed of this. Can you decipher what I'm saying?" inquired Sheetal.

"I already know the solution, but since it was your dream, you should decipher it," Kiran grinned.

"I was perplexed about it, but now I have a crystal clear answer. I found my ray of light. His name is Kiran, who erased the darkness from my life," said Sheetal.

"Coincidentally, the name Kiran means a ray of light," remarked Kiran.

"Destiny is real." And at first, I believed you were a pervert, so I loathed you," Sheetal remarked.

It's typical for me that people initially perceive me as a pervert, but once they learn more about who I really am, they will see that it was a contradiction. I consider myself to be a friendly person. At first, the majority of my female friends misinterpreted me. They then expressed regret for their error," Kiran said.

"Oh, I see," Sheetal replied.

"So, do you mind if I have friends who are women?" inquired Kiran.

Sheetal raised an eyebrow.

"I inquired about this because a number of my friends had girlfriends that forbade them from speaking with other women. They fight about little things, hehe," Kiran remarked innocently.

Since I have trust in you, I don't see any issues with that. You are a gentleman. You've never acted inappropriately towards me," Sheetal remarked with a genuine smile."

Kiran responded, "I admire this character in you."

"I never mixed well with anyone, which is why I don't have friends," Sheetal complained.

"Don't worry, you will get it. Go ahead, I'm excited," Kiran said.

"I began to think of you when I saw that awful dream. I made an effort to ignore these thoughts, but I was unable. You know, you were thrilled when we went to the giant wheel. Your face looked so adorable and charming at that moment. With her dazzling eyes, Sheetal exclaimed, "I couldn't stop staring at your cuteness!"

"Am I cute? Kiran remarked, "I'm not a kid.

"You are indeed a man, and you're really cute. Additionally, you shined and were delightful while we went boating. Sheetal said, "Your smile melted my cold heart."

"Unbelievable. You admired me. Why then did you not own up to it? Inquiringly, Kiran asked.

"Kiara arrived right as I was going to confess in the restaurant. Sheetal sighed, "You know how I felt when you said like she's interested and you were shy."

"You had concealed all of these feelings and covered them up with a smile. "Why?" inquired Kiran.

"Because I want you to be happy." Although I disliked pretending, I did it because I thought she was more attractive than me and my character was mundane. You were deeply in love with her. I believed that I was the issue. I decided to stand by you all and never show up in your lives again. Sheetal had tears in her eyes.

After wiping her tears, Kiran put his palms over her face and expressed his regret for what she had to endure. Furthermore, Kiara isn't superior to you. To me, you are always lovely."

Kiran added, "Unlike you, Kiara's character is phoney. You are sincere. Despite your icy exterior, I am sure you have a good soul."

"I'm glad you came into my life," Sheetal replied.

Kiran offered his hand to her.

They clasped their hands.

They gazed intently into their eyes.

Captivated by one other, their gazes met.

The cry of a baby startled them.

They returned to the realm of reality.

They let go of what they had done and laughed.

"We act like teenagers even though we are in our 30s." We might be cringing," Sheetal remarked.

"Love is blind, and we might act crinkly, but at least we're happy," Kiran grinned. To be honest, the term cringe killed a lot of cute actions. Sometimes people's fear of being classified as cringe prevents them from even portraying their true selves."

"Why do we need to be afraid if our actions don't harm someone?" Sheetal questioned.

Kiran retorted, "Exactly. What's the plan for us?

After giving it some thought, Sheetal responded, "We should speak with our parents. We don't have to get married right away. I'm hoping you get it."

"I know you have left-over work at the office, and I need some time to adjust to my new job and also we need to know us more," Kiran replied.

"Exactly, and do you think your parents will approve of our relationship?" Sheetal enquired.

"I believe they might agree. They were not delighted that I was living a solitary life, to be honest. And one individual will undoubtedly encourage our relationship, Kiran added.

"Your brother?" Sheetal enquired.

Indeed, what about you? inquired Kiran.

They have no reason for rejecting our relationship. Aside from that, we are not very young," Sheetal remarked.

"Yeah, that's a fact," he stated.

Sheetal questioned, "Are you feeling sleepy?"

Kiran gave a nod.

"You can sleep if you'd like by resting your head on my shoulder," she added.

Kiran's gaze expanded.

Kiran responded, "Thank you, but I think you might be tired."

"I don't feel sleepy at all. You can sleep for an hour now.

Resting his head on her shoulders, Kiran drifted off to sleep. He was tired since he hadn't slept at all yesterday due to his excitement and anxiety over today.

Sheetal gave his head a gentle rub.

The plane landed down on Trivandrum.

After getting off the plane, our travel companions met Keerthan and Nihal.

"I'm glad to meet you, brother," Keerthan hugged Kiran.

"Sheetal, this is my bro Keerthan and his friend Nihal," Kiran said, looking bewildered. And this Sheetal."

Kiran was suspicious of Keerthan and Nihal's happiness.

They made their way to the vehicle.

"Nice to meet you guys," Sheetal remarked, "and I'm going."

"We will drop you," Kiran murmured.

"It must be hard for," Sheetal remarked.

It's our obligation, Sister, Keerthan said.

"Obligation?" Sheetal and Kiran questioned.

Nihal grinned nervously and replied, "Nothing. He was just too enthusiastic. Kindly get in the car, Kiran bro and sis."

Nihal pulled open the door.

They were inside now.

Keerthan was the driver of the car. Sheetal led the way.

The car was driven by Keerthan.

Sheetal directed the way.

They arrived at her house.

"Thank you, and could you please come to my house?" inquired Sheetal.

"Your sis-in-law is inviting us to meet her parents," Nihal whispered to Keerthan.

"Why not?" Keerthan asked.

"I am looking so exhausted," Kiran remarked.

"We are not going for an interview, bro," Nihal remarked. She's making a request. You can go, and so can we.

They got out of the vehicle and proceeded to her residence.

After unlocking the gate, Sheetal proceeded to the doorbell.

She pressed the doorbell.

Upon opening the door, her parents were taken aback to see her daughter. Seeing her pleased face made them very happy. She had given them hugs.

Nihal, Kiran, and Keerthan were present to see this.

"I apologise. I forgot to introduce them," Sheetal remarked. It's Kiran here.

Sheetal's dad said, "You are Kiran, her travel companion."

Kiran nodded.

Sheetal continued, "This is Keerthan, his brother and Nihal, Keerthan's friend. They came here to pick up Kiran."

Sheetal's mom said, "Children, why are you standing here on the doorstep? Come inside."

They came inside.

"Your sister-in-law's house and parents are good, I guess," Nihal whispered.

Keerthan smiled.

They were seated on chairs.

Sheetal's dad said, "Kiran, how was the interview?"

Sheetal smiled.

Kiran said, "I got the job."

Sheetal's dad said, "That's great. Congrats."

Kiran expressed gratitude.

Sheetal's father inquired, "What are you guys doing?"

"I'm a neurologist," Keerthan declared.

Nihal replied, "I work as an interior designer."

"Excellent," said Sheetal's father.

Sheetal's mother had by then brought tea and snacks.

They finished it off.

"Where are you coming from?" Sheetal's mother enquired.

"Kollam," Kiran murmured.

"Kiran, thank you for making her happy," Sheetal's mother stated. She has changed, as we can see. God bless you for returning our daughter.

"Mom, don't get emotional," Sheetal remarked.

"Sorry, Uncle and Aunty, but we have to go now," Keerthan remarked.

Yes, I can understand that you guys can leave," Sheetal's father remarked.

However, you can visit our house. "We are not strangers," Sheetal's mother added.

They smiled.

They got up and left.

"I thought youngsters these days are spoiled ones," Sheetal's father remarked. These men are determined.

"Mom of Sheetal nodded.

Within the vehicle, Nihal and Keerthan were pleased with Kiran and Sheetal.

Kiran, meanwhile, was staring at the moon and contemplating about his journey.

"Why is the moon so beautiful?" he wondered.

They arrived in Kollam.

CHAPTER XXV

BACK TO REGULAR LIVES

Even though our travel companion had gone back to their regular routines, life had grown more exquisite for them.

Sheetal had escaped from her dark and empty days.

After two weeks, she went back to the bank.

Her co-worker noticed a change in her facial expression. She usually showed up with a neutral expression and no smile on her face. However, she was smiling now and wished the majority of the employees a good morning.

She first went to Ganga and expressed her gratitude for managing her work.

"Welcome," Ganga said.

Then she went to see the Manager to inform him that she was back.

Her happiness and excellent nature also astounded Sachin.

During the lunch break,

Sheetal headed to the area where her co-workers typically sat down to eat lunch together after packing her lunch.

Sheetal said, "Can I join with you guys?"

After a brief moment of shock, they cheerfully let her sit among them.

"I'm grateful," Sheetal stated.

An awkward silence fell.

After giving them all a glance, Sheetal asked, "Did I disrupt your conversations?"

"No, we never expected such pleasant behaviour from you," Sajan retorted.

With a smile, Sheetal answered, "I get it. I am aware that you all put up with my harsh and stoic demeanour. I'm sorry for being such a cold-hearted lady.

They accepted her apology in full.

"What is the reason for your positive change?" Yamuna asked.

With a smile, Sheetal said, "My journey." I'd realised my mistakes and decided to fix them. Before the journey, I had disconnected from the people around me and had forgotten how to live. At present, I have changed and I am trying to socialize.

"We are glad you have changed and are pleased now," Yadav remarked.

Sheetal grinned. "May I ask one question, please?" Ganga inquired.

Sheetal answered, "Yes."

"You are certain that the right person entered your life?" asked Ganga.

Sheetal responded, "Yes, you guys follow my Instagram account, right?" with a quick blush.

"Yes, we do," replied Yamuna.

"His name is Kiran," stated Sheetal. Our meeting was so unexpected that we unintentionally ended up as travel companions. He's been a major part of my transformation.

"Love will make changes," remarked Yadav.

After finishing their lunches, they returned to their works

Sheetal took her bike to Ivory Crust Enterprises in the evening and waited for someone.

Kiran arrived.

They both smiled.

"May I take you to a tea shop?" declared Kiran.

"You've been familiar with this place for just one day? Fantastic," Sheetal exclaimed.

"I typically have a cup of tea in the evening. "I've found the perfect store," Kiran said.

"Alright, I'll drop you off there," winked Sheetal.

Kiran responded, "This is your bike. Pretty good."

Sheetal answered, "Yeah, and I didn't let anyone drive or give left from this bike."

Kiran asked, "Can I?" with a gentle shake of his head.

With a smile, Sheetal responded, "Of course."

Kiran appreciated Sheetal's driving skills and later he pointed out the spot.

It was a tea shop that also provided snacks. An elderly couple owned and operated the majestic-looking building. The elderly couple serving tea in cups was seated on wooden seats in the tea store.

These days, the majority of hotels adhere to a specific design that is reminiscent of Western customs. While many people cherish their traditional lifestyle, the majority of people prefer modernity.

The appearance of the tea shop brought back fond memories for our travel companions.

They placed two onion vadas and two tea orders.

"Kiran, although having lived here for thirty years, I have never taken notice of this spot. I'm sorry, I missed this. I had the impression of returning to my early years. This tea smells great, and the vada tastes delicious. I have no words to express how I'm feeling right now," Sheetal added, her expression pleasant.

Yes, we may neglect to notice the outside world most of the time. "By the way, I have a question for you," Kiran remarked.

Sheetal nodded as she consumed the snack.

"God's sake, my office and your bank are close by, but we're both too busy working on our jobs. Let's spend our evenings together if that is possible. Just an hour from 5 PM -6 PM. We may discuss our days for an hour, which strengthens our relationship and helps us talk about our days," Kiran stated solemnly.

It's a wise idea. It's an hour we can keep for ourselves. How was your first day, then?" Sheetal enquired.

"That's okay, but I promise I'll have an abundance of work, so I'll give it my best." I should have thanked your father for arranging my accommodation, too," Kiran remarked.

He was helping his future son-in-law right now. "Have you discussed our relationship with your parents?" inquired Sheetal.

Kiran gave a nod.

"What did they say?", asked Sheetal.

"My father mentioned that he needed to look into your family background and whereabouts. Kiran said, "My mum is ready to accept you as my wife because she likes you."

"I assumed your mother would consider me a haughty woman since most aunts judge me," Sheetal remarked.

"She differs from those individuals. Keerthan once showed her the picture we had taken in Munnar. And she told me once, "I wanted to take care of you, even though you looked happy in the photo, you might have been hiding your worries." Besides, that was before I developed feelings for you," Kiran said.

"That's good to know," Sheetal responded with an authentic smile.

"What about your parents?" enquired Kiran.

"My dad predicted you are the person, and they said the same answer that your father did," declared Sheetal.

Kiran inquired, "How was your experience today?"

"My behaviour shocked everyone, even our manager Sachin sir. I also shared our meal with my co-worker for the first time when we sat down to eat. They were so kind to me," Sheetal exclaimed in response.

Kiran noticed the joy glimmering in her eyes. "I am happy about you, dear," he remarked, casting a glance at it.

"Don't gaze upon me like that," Sheetal remarked. I will melt if you continue this.

"You don't realise how beautiful your eyes are when you're excited," Kiran remarked.

"And you don't know how beautiful is your smile," Sheetal remarked.

"Thank you," Kiran murmured in a cute voice.

"Well, I regret all the years I wasted," Sheetal said.

"Past is past, just live your present," commented Kiran.

According to Sheetal, "I believe that most people are aware that we are in love because of our posts and stories."

"Most of my friends are now asking for treats after congratulating me, hehe. Kiran laughed and said, "I was the one who insisted they give treats whenever they got into relationships."

Sheetal remarked, "Karma is a boomerang child."

Kiran said, "But my karma is adorable."

"So, throw a party," Sheetal said.

"I am not rich. I had travelled with all of my savings," Kiran remarked.

"It's the same. I have to start over lol, but the trip was valuable," Sheetal added.

Kiran retorted, "I believe we ought to check out Santhosh George Kulangara's books for proper money management before our next trip."

"Yes, and I believe that we should leave. How quickly the time had passed", Sheetal exclaimed.

"Time is going to fly by if we spend it with our loved ones," Kiran retorted.

Sheetal grinned.

They made the payment.

They observed the elderly couple busy in the works in the shop.

He said, "When we get older like them, we can open a tea shop like this."

"Excellent," she replied.

Sheetal dropped him at his hostel and waved her hands.

This schedule made them both pleasant

CHAPTER XXVI

LOVE AND HURT

They had successfully passed their three-month relationship. They were happy that their families had accepted their relationship.

Their hectic schedules prevented them from spending as much time together as other couples. They met in the old couple's tea shop every evening of the working day.

They discussed various subjects and had various snacks. They talked about their embarrassing, bittersweet, and joyous childhood memories and shared their opinions about various topics.

Kiran spoke a lot most of the time, and Sheetal listened to him. He was full of topics to talk about. Kiran was excited to engage in conversation with Sheetal, who appreciated his constant talking.

The shop typically gets crowded in the morning and evening with people coming in to drink tea, catch up with friends or lovers, or just take in the atmosphere and listen to the classic radio music.

The old couple used to talk with them in their free time.

Kiran and Sheetal liked to listen to their conversations about their hardships, love, and life.

Kiran knew Sheetal's friends and coworkers, and she knew his coworkers as well due to their daily conversations.

It is rather typical for a couple to quarrel in a relationship. These arguments give the relationship a more realistic feeling.

Additionally, following a single altercation, the pair will attempt to rectify their errors.

Some arguments, however, may destroy these beautiful relationships, and the couples will grow apart to the point that they will never unite again. It's referred to as a breakup.

As a result, love—the most exquisite emotion—becomes an unhealed trauma.

One fine evening, Sheetal spent more than ten minutes at Ivory Crust's office waiting for Kiran. He did not show up. She gave him many calls.

At last, he returned her call. The time was 5:30 PM.

She picked it.

"Hi Kiran, how are you doing? I am waiting in front of your workplace. Come on, let's head out."

"I apologise, but I have a lot of work to finish."

"It's okay, but please let me know ahead of time so I can save time."

"Take care and bye."

And he disconnected the call.

Sheetal felt disappointed. Later on, she knew that was because he would be busy.

She texted him the following morning asking if he could come in the evening.

A few hours later, he texted

"I apologise; I have an extremely busy agenda this week. I can't be with you. I'll probably finish my work in a week. I love you, dear."

In response, Sheetal texted back, *"Okay, do your best."*

Sheetal missed him and her parents noted that. They questioned her about why her unique sparkle had vanished.

She also informed me of Kiran's busy schedule.

She listened to their advice and decided to exercise patience.

After one week:-

When she arrived at work one day; she noticed that Yamuna, one of her coworkers, was crying and that her coworkers were consoling her.

"What is the issue?" Sheetal asked.

"Join me here. I'll tell you about it, Ganga answered.

Sheetal accompanied Ganga.

"Are you knowledgeable of her relationship?" inquired Ganga

With a game developer, that is, correct? He is a pleasant man. We have spoken with him before.

Ganga said, "This pleasant man cheated her."

How come? Sheetal was astonished to hear that "We all saw him treat her well, and he was a good-mannered guy."

He possesses great acting skills. Ganga remarked, "He had built a wall of lies about himself.

"This is unbelievable. What, then, is his purpose? inquired Sheetal.

Ganga remarked, "He was a sadist who just played with her feelings.

" Yamana is an innocent and good-hearted individual. Sheetal said, "I feel bad for her.

"Men are untrustworthy." Their acting is impressive. We have no idea what's going through their heads", said Ganga.

Sheetal was empty. She pondered Kiran's most recent transformation.

Hey, I just mentioned that. Keep it in perspective.

Ganga patted her shoulders and murmured, "Alright."

Sheetal forced a grin.

She was browsing Instagram during her lunch break.

She viewed a story of Sajan, one of her fellow workers.

It was an image of him and his pals attending a friend's birthday celebration in a pub.

All was well until she saw a familiar face in a white shirt filling a glass with liquor.

The man matched Kiran's exact resemblance.

Since his spectacles were identical, she could confirm that it was Kiran.

She reached her home.

When Mom saw her face, she said, "What happened, dear?"

"Nothing Mom, I am having a headache," she smiled.

"Oh, I see, apply balm and sleep," her mother remarked. Your work may be causing you to get headaches. I'm happy that tomorrow is a holiday.

With a nod, Sheetal went to her room and shut the door.

She wasn't ready to share bout her sadness with anyone. She turned on the fan and turned it up to full speed.

She approached the almirah's mirror.

She glanced at her mirror.

She put her fist in the mirror and folded it. She wept, pressing her face against her fist.

She declared:

"I can't believe that he deceived me. I thought God showed mercy towards me, but it wasn't. I am unable to bear this torture. I had complete faith and affection for him, but what did he give back?

Why are men all the same way?

How am I going to rid myself of all those lovely memories of him?

How will I tell my parents that I made the wrong decision?"

She let out a cry while covering her mouth.

She abruptly got a notification.

Grabbing the phone, she verified that it was a text message from Kiran.

"Finally, my hectic schedule has come to an end. I sincerely missed having you here. We can get together in the park at 9 a.m. tomorrow since it's a holiday."

Anger had replaced her sadness.

She decided to call him to end this and bit her teeth to do so.

Later, she decided to end their relationship completely by meeting him the following day.

She sent a text.

"Alright."

She took a bath, went to eat dinner, and returned to her room.

She sobbed because she had trouble falling asleep. After all, she had been thinking about all of their wonderful times together.

CHAPTER XXVII

THE UNLUCKY ROSE

Sheetal was an early riser.

For a little moment, she didn't even close her eyelashes.

She grabbed her bike and got ready.

Riding the bike brought up memories for Kiran, so Sheetal did her best not to cry.

When she arrived at the park at 8:45, she sat down on a bench.

There weren't as many people in the park as she had anticipated.

She found a vacant bench and seated.

She was sitting erect, gazing towards the sky.

There was hardly a hint of sunlight; the sky was full of dark clouds.

Lost in her agonising thoughts, she prepared her mind to endure the pain.

Kiran showed up a few minutes later.

Since he arrived there after nine o'clock, he was sprinting.

He ran to her bench after finding it.

"I apologise for being late, Sheetal," he answered.

Sheetal rose from the chair.

"I'm not sure why, but I think the weather is unpleasant today. Veiled in ominous clouds and appearing so gloomy," Kiran remarked, glancing up at the sky.

Sheetal did not look at him or answer his words.

"What happened to you?" Kiran said while glaring her eyes. You have such tired-looking eyes. Avoid overstressing yourself.

Ignoring him, Sheetal answered, "Nothing to panic about."

"Hey, why do you refuse to interact with me? I see why you were feeling so grumpy. He apologised gently. "I'm sorry, beloved, I wasn't able to talk to you or meet you these days.

He went into his pocket, grabbed a bright red rose, and offered it to her.

Kiran said, "Darling, please talk to me."

Sheetal stared at him and then rose, turning her head in the middle of it.

"How can you act like this perfectly?" she questioned.

After a brief moment of confusion, Kiran responded, "Don't tease me, and just take this flower?"

With a smile, Sheetal accepted the rose flower.

Kiran remarked, "After finishing a lot of work at my office, I am finally relieved I could meet you."

"When did Ivory Crust become a pub?" inquired Sheetal.

Kiran's expression had gone from content to frighten.

Kiran answered, "Sheetal..." I'll explain.

When Sheetal lost her temper, she furiously threw the rose to the ground.

Taking out her phone, Sheetal showed her a screenshot of Sajan's Instagram story picture, which featured Kiran sitting there and filling a glass with alcohol.

Kiran's tension was reflected in his eyes.

"You told me once that you are a teetotaller because your dad was a drunkard," Sheetal had stated angrily. Then who the hell is filling the cups with liquor?"

Sheetal, I wanna talk to you," Kiran asked.

"What, talk to me? You have a great talent for telling tales in a flash. "I bet you have plenty of stories," exclaimed Sheetal.

Tears were streaming from her eyes. She cleaned those.

"You are a liar!" she cried at him, pointing. You had been lying to me from the very beginning. You initially said you were unfamiliar with Munnar when we got lost in the forests, but in reality, it was your second visit. Then you deceived the public; we are a married couple.

"Sheetal, please don't misunderstand me. Please hear me out," requested him.

"I don't want to listen to your ridiculously made-up stories. She shouted, "And justified, it was for a surprise."

Kiran held her hands together and said, "Please don't overthink, dear."

"Dear? Who knows? Maybe you asked her if you could get back together and she rejected you away. And you have to consider me as a backup plan and if she comes back you probably ditch me," exclaimed Sheetal.

With a boiled-blooded reply, Kiran said, "SHUT UP, and don't make assumptions."

"You became enraged. That is all. "Your lies are not as bitter as the truth," Sheetal declared.

"I can't tolerate your wrong assumptions. You are not a secondary concern. I had indeed loved her once, but it doesn't mean that I hate you. Now my heart is beating for you and I can't deliberately hurt you, Kiran continued, "And please trust me," his eyes welling up with tears.

"Acting is nice," Sheetal cheered. You breached my trust in you. Since you are a liar and a disloyal person, I will quit loving you, even though I can't stop myself. I am not even able to believe your mere words.

Please give me a chance, Sheetal. I'd like to clarify," he pleaded.

A tiny droplet had dropped to the ground from the gloomy clouds, and it had begun to rain hard. It was pouring with atmosphere.

"Let's break up, Kiran. She sobbed, getting her tears mixed up with raindrops, "I can't stay in a relationship with a deceiver."

After hearing her, his whole world shattered into a million pieces.

Devastated, Kiran dropped to his knees.

Sheetal turned away from him and began to move.

"Sheetal, please hear me out!" he yelled. I'm begging you. I don't tell lies.

You will always remain a painful memory for my mind and an unhealed wound in my heart," she replied, stopping.

The strong rain witnessed this agonising scene.

The bright red rose in the ground is no longer there since the soil and rain caused it to lose its lovely scent and beauty.

CHAPTER XXVIII

REALITY HITS

Kiran rose from the ground. All he could do was watch as she slowly faded from his view. He ran towards a shed since it was raining a lot. In the shed, he was by himself.

He sensed that the rain's beauty was gone. Rain usually made him feel happy and fulfilled, but right now it's simply tears and sadness from somebody.

It was raining when Sheetal rode her bike. She found it difficult to accept the reality of things.

When she arrived home, her parents were surprised to see their daughter soaking wet from the rain. Grabbing a towel, her mother gave Sheetal a head rub.

Sheetal was lost, thus she was unable to hear her parents talking.

"We had a breakup," she added. Do not question me about this, please.

They were startled. Sheetal made her way upstairs to her room.

Her dad stopped her mom before she could follow her, saying, "Dear, all she wants is time." We wish not to irritate her. And when the time is appropriate, we can speak with her, alright?

She gave a nod.

Kiran arrived at his rental house. He showered and changed out of his drenched clothes. After that, he napped and consumed medication for a cold fever.

Kiran's family and friends were thrilled with his relationship; therefore, he wasn't ready to tell anyone. He wasn't prepared to ruin their joy.

On the evening of the following day, he went to meet her at the bank.

When Sheetal noticed him, she led him to a spot that was empty so that her colleagues wouldn't see them.

Before Kiran could say something, she stated, "If you try to talk to me, I will surely file a complaint against you."

The words had penetrated his heart as sharply as a knife.

Kiran understood all had gone when Sheetal finally regarded him like a nuisance.

On holidays, Kiran pretended to be busy with his mother and avoided going home. He used to lie to her whenever she asked about Sheetal, claiming that she was also busy and so on.

Sheetal kept the breakup a secret from her co-workers.

Their professional lives were unaffected by their breakup. They both believed that their careers offered an escape from their heartbreak.

Yamuna was in Sheetal's office, having, with Yadav's support, overcome her toxic relationship. He was a kind man who had a one-sided love for her. But Yadav hesitated from confessing because Yamuna had a lover. However, Yadav sensed bad energy from her ex-boyfriend. Yes, that was accurate. Yadav and Yamuna have now committed, and they will shortly get engaged.

Sheetal's mind would fly back to Kiran whenever she saw them. "It was a sweet nightmare," she thought.

Though Sheetal was unable to but pretended to despise Kiran.

For Kiran, this meant that he frequently dreamed of Sheetal accusing him of lying.

It has now been a month since the breakup.

They thought this month had been too long.

Their way of life had evolved.

They missed their daily chats, their regular meetings, the tea store, the tea, and even true happiness.

They tended to go through the various pictures they had taken, both before and after their relationship began.

Their love was their final hope for survival.

They found it difficult to bear the hurt of the split.

""Love is the most beautiful feeling, however, it also causes the most pain.""

CHAPTER XXIX

WHEN DOCTOR BECAME MEDIATOR

Keerthan paid a surprise visit to Kiran's home one day.

Kiran was shocked to see him and worried that Keerthan would surely detect through his heartbreak.

Keerthan is staying with Kiran while in a three-day medical camp in Trivandrum.

"This house is affordable with good facilities," Keerthan remarked after taking a look at his rental home. I like the choice made by your father-in-law.

Kiran gave an awkward smile.

"Well, I will accompany you to meet Sheetal sis in the evening, sis," Keerthan remarked.

"No, you can't," Kiran replied in shock.

I'll ride your bike by myself, so don't worry. With a mischievous smile, Keerthan declared, "I want to meet her no matter what."

"No, you just can't, and move on," Kiran yelled.

"Bro, you can't hide your grief with anger?" Keerthan remarked, giving Kiran a stern look and an honest grin.

Kiran's expression changed abruptly.

"You haven't visited our house in a month," Keerthan went on. Although your acting abilities may fool our innocent mother into believing you are alright, I can tell there is a problem with you.

"No, I was stressed because of my hectic schedule, nothing more," Kiran responded.

"Don't lie to me, Kiran. Please tell me what transpired between you and her, inquired seriously, Keerthan.

Startled, Kiran enquired, "How do you know?"

"We have the same blood, lol," Keerthan remarked with a smile. I always bother you, but I'll be there for you if you need me.

Tears filled Kiran's eyes. He kept their breakup a secret from everyone.

Everything that occurred between Kiran revealed them to Keerthan.

"Both sides made mistakes," Keerthan stated. She misinterpreted you, and you were unable to clarify this to her.

Kiran answered, "She threatened to sue me if I spoke with her.

"Can't blame her too," Keerthan remarked. Are you willing to speak with her now?

Without a doubt. Kiran remarked, "I gave up because I thought I was bothering her."

I'll make an effort to set up a meeting with her. And you ought to make use of it," Keerthan remarked.

"May I ask what your plan is?" Kiran enquired.

"Give me her phone number", commanded Keerthan.

Kiran added, "She will cut off the call if she discovers your identity."

"Relax and have patience," Keerthan answered.

Keerthan grabbed his phone and gave her a call.

After finishing her lunch, Sheetal received this call. It was an unidentified no. She relocated to a space and went there.

"Hey, who's that?"

"Hello, sis. My name is Keerthan.

"Oh, I don't want any explanations. It's over now.

" Please don't get upset with me, sister. And I called you to ask that you not support my brother.

"Then."

"Regret is a slow poison, sis. He will regret not having the opportunity to share his perspective, and you might regret not hearing it in the future."

"I refuse to pay attention to his false stories."

"Sis I am pleading just to listen to what he has to say."

"What do you want me to understand?"

"Well, may we meet up at 5 p.m. in the public park?"

"I'm not sure."

"Sis, this isn't just for him—I'm setting this up for the two of you too."

"All right, I'll be there."

"Sis, thank you very much."

The call was cut off.

Kiran stood close to him. What she said, he inquired.

"She's coming," Keerthan promised.

Kiran hugged him and whispered, "You are my precious brother."

"Stop soaping," Keerthan stated. I'm not sure if she will accept your forgiveness.

"I just want to confess to her what had happened," Kiran replied. That is all. So why should we pick the same spot? It's the same unfortunate spot where everything was destroyed.

"We're able to fix it," Keerthan remarked.

In the public park at 5:00 p.m.,

"Is it possible that she will come?" inquired Kiran.

"She could," Keerthan replied.

"Look at how gloomy the weather is. Just like that day," Kiran hesitantly answered.

"Did you bring an umbrella?" inquired Keerthan.

Kiran yelled, "Your umbrella. I am worried about my future."

"My future worries me as well. She is your future, my health is my future. Same but distinct, Keerthan said.

"What if she lied to you?" Kiran questioned.

"We're heading back to your place," Keerthan immediately answered.

"You are so pessimistic," Kiran remarked.

Keerthan remarked, "Complaining about the location and climate is an example of your optimism."

"See, she's approaching." We saw her," Keerthan remarked.

Wearing his glasses, Kiran endeavoured to locate her. He saw her.

Her hair had grown a bit, and he could see a hint of despair on her face.

Keerthan sarcastically said, "I see the joy of your breakup reflected on both of your faces."

"I am sorry about her," Kiran murmured.

"Well, you should utilise the chance she had given," Keerthan retorted. All you have to do is yourself, and if you are sincere, she will accept you.

"I am sincere," Kiran declared.

Keerthan wished all the best to him.

Upon hearing their murmurs, Sheetal reached forward to meet them.

Sheetal was unable to maintain eye contact with Kiran.

"Hello sis," Keerthan remarked as he extended his hand to shake hers.

She accepted his handshake and smiled uneasily.

Keerthan gave Kiran a fierce look and made a calm motion.

"So you guys may proceed. I have an urgent call," Keerthan went.

An awkward silence fell.

They were both staring at the floor.

"Can I speak?" Kiran inquired, breaking the ice.

When Sheetal heard his question. She was rather taken aback. They had become strangers.

They were formal in their interactions. They understood there was a distance between them.

"Yes," Sheetal replied.

With a sigh, Kiran fixed his gaze on Sheetal's eyes and spoke, "I will tell you exactly what had happened those days."

Sheetal stared at him attentively.

"Our company had a build a home for a client," he said. Unfortunately, a few years later, the house underwent damage. It was Ivory Crust's first-ever complaint. Our company employees contacted the customer and made a fair compensation offer. However, he intended to sue our business and wasn't prepared for the money.

"What are you trying to say?" inquired Sheetal.

Please be patient, Kiran pleaded.

Sheetal gave a nod.

"Our company's reputation will suffer if he files a lawsuit. Because he was a sadist, he refused to turn down legitimate compensation. Ganesh sir gave me the charge of convincing him. He had faith in my ability to persuade."

After a little period of silence, Kiran said, "This man was an alcoholic frequenter of bars and pubs, but he was going through financial difficulties. He had no one to rule, as he was single and had no family or obligations."

"So you went to the pub to meet him, then why were you pouring spirits into the glass?" inquired Sheetal.

I went to the exact pubs and bars he went to in those days," Kiran remarked. I got to know him. We had conversations, and I took care of his bills. I never drank those, even though I frequented pubs and bars. Usually, I would chat with him and order lemon juice.

Then what occurred? Sheetal enquired.

Kiran stated, "I had been honest with him and let him know that accepting the offer and giving up drinking would be beneficial for his health and wealth. For god's sake, he had signed the contract and taken the payment. He is currently at a rehabilitation facility. Our organisation identified the reason and increased its construction vigilance.

"Why do you hide all of these?" Sheetal questioned.

"I can't reveal this before the settlement," Kiran remarked. I decided to speak about this after the settlement. You misinterpreted me and were furious with me.

His eyes were sincere, and Sheetal saw that he was honest.

Kiran went on, "Sheetal, trust is the most important component in a relationship. I want to eliminate any suspicions you may have right now. I had already explained the incident involving the jungle safari. If I said that I am coming here for the second time, then you will concentrate and we will end up lost. I get lost all the time."

Sheetal gave a nod.

"In the instance of fabricating our marital status to appease the elderly couple, I was helpless to refute their assumption and, more crucially. About Kiara, It was she who requested to restart the relationship. It's also true that I lied to surprise you. I wanted to make your day unforgettable", remarked Kiran.

Sheetal shed regretful tears in her eyes.

Kiran glared straight into her eyes and said, "She was my first crush, but you are my last love. Always remember that.

Keerthan was watching the entire scene away from them under a tree. He was curious about them.

That's all, Kiran said. I appreciate your time, and at this point, you can decide whether to believe me. I want the best for you in the future, Sheetal, and goodbye.

Just as Kiran turned to walk away, Sheetal grabbed his wrist.

Hold on to me. I'll be back in a short while," she remarked.

She sprinted away from his hand.

Keerthan asked over his phone to Kiran.

"What took place? Why did she flee?"

"I'm not sure."

"What would happen if she called the police?"

"Shut up. And you, where were you?"

"Even though I am far away, I can still see you guys."

Keerthan got a call and he walked away.

Abruptly, there was some faint drizzle.

Negative ideas rushed across Kiran's mind.

"Similar location and weather also bring back memories of that melancholy day. What if this is the beginning of something terrible?"

Sheetal returned a little while later.

With her right hand concealing something, she started sprinting in his direction.

Keerthan was witnessing the entire scene standing behind the tree and he couldn't understand what was going on.

With a passionate gaze towards Kiran, Sheetal knelt and presented a *magnificent bouquet of blue roses*.

Kiran was speechless, and Keerthan was staring open-mouthed.

Sheetal cried out, "Please forgive me. I promise you that I will do all in my capacity to keep our lines of communication open. Accept my apology, please."

Kiran took the bouquet.

The drizzling made the scene more beautiful.

Sheetal lifted herself off the ground.

"Can we restart our relationship and make it eternal?" said Sheetal.

Kiran looked at her gravely.

"Are you still angry at me?" inquired Sheetal.

With a smile, Kiran gave her an unexpected hug and spun her around. She experienced a sense of flight.

They were both extremely pleased about it.

Their agony was no longer felt.

Their hearts reconnected, and this time, it was forever.

When Keerthan witnessed the scene, he was ecstatic.

He admired them.

"Kiran dismissed me. Sheetal laughed and remarked, "This is a park, and Keerthan is laughing."

Kiran set her down. I apologise if you are feeling dizzy.

"I loved it even though I feel dizzy", said Sheetal shyly.

Her cheeks were flushed.

Keerthan came over to them.

Sheetal and Kiran became shy.

"Don't need to be shy. I saw your beautiful romance. Well, sis, I never expected you would buy a bouquet for him. Usually, men do that.

"Men deserve flowers too, and this blue bouquet represents my apology and love," Sheetal grinned. The colour blue represents forgiveness.

Keerthan remarked, "Wonderful, I admire you guys and Kiran. I never expected you to be this much stronger."

Kiran flexed his arms.

Sheetal said, "Bro, I don't know how to thank you for your help."

Nevermind. Keerthan answered, "All I want is you guys to be happy and never make this mistake again."

They agreed.

"I am at a loss for words. You repaired this even though you've never been in a relationship. How? asked Kiran.

With a smirk, Keerthan remarked, "Coaches don't play."

"Then be a permanent coach?" Kiran asked.

"No, I'll marry someone after your marriage," Keerthan replied.

"We won't get married anytime soon," Kiran declared.

"You ought to get married soon," Keerthan retorted.

"Hey, stop it," Sheetal uttered.

Okay, there is no appeal if the sister-in-law gives the order. I'm taking your bike, Kiran. We can visit your tea shop, Keerthan suggested.

Sheetal and Kiran went on a bike ride together after a month.

Keerthan glanced at his empty rear seat, hoping one day his lover would eventually take a seat there.

They arrived at the tea shop.

When Keerthan saw the store, he was ecstatic. "Pure nostalgic," he remarked.

At the time of their arrival, the elderly couple was free.

The elderly couple asked about their one-month absence. The elderly couple remarked, "It's normal to have disputes in a relationship but always think every problem has a solution," when they told them about the incident.

Keerthan also warmed up to the elderly couple.

That day, our travel companions realised that communication is essential to maintaining a positive relationship. The misunderstandings will fade away with effective communication.

Thus strengthening and enhancing the relationship.

CHAPTER XXX

EUPHORIA

Two months later, in Angelina's beauty salon.

Sheetal went to the same employees with whom she had acted harshly that day.

The staff was going to give Angelina a call.

Sheetal apologised for what had occurred that day.

"It's okay, ma'am," the worker said with a smile.

When Angelina arrived, she was startled to find Sheetal. "You haven't come to get your hair trimmed in six months. What took place?"

"It's a long story," answered Sheetal with a smile. I did, however, choose to grow my hair out.

With a humorous reply, Angelina said, "We lost our frequent customer."

"So sad, but I came here to know about the rate of an engagement makeup," Sheetal remarked.

"Oh my gosh, I've finally comprehended the plot of the long story. Congratulations dear," remarked an ecstatic Angelina.

Indeed, guys, the engagement of our travel companions had been arranged.

They ceremoniously exchanged rings on the day of their engagement.

On that day, their marriage date was also fixed. Coincidently, it was the same date they met for the first time in Munnar.

Because he had to wait six months to attend their wedding, Keerthan was the only one who wasn't fond of the date.

Drawing inspiration from their journey, Kiran began writing a novel titled 'My Travel Companion.'

He struggled to strike a balance between writing and office employment.

Three months later, his book was published.

Kiran dedicated his novel to Sheetal.

Surprisingly, his novel was well accepted by the people. The plot was the book's primary attraction. A genre that is uplifting and suitable for all ages. Nonetheless, he was subjected to criticism from individuals who held distaste for the light-hearted novel genre. But many people truly appreciated his book.

Kiran was in his bed one Sunday. An unknown number called him. He answered the phone. When his publisher contacted him, he extended an invitation to attend the publishing house's award event, where his novel received the prize for 'the best debut novel.'

Kiran experienced a state of euphoria. He informed his family of this information.

He considered calling Sheetal to tell her but then changed his mind. When they next met at the tea shop, he decided to tell her about his award.

In the tea store, they were drinking tea.

"Sheetal, I won an award in the best debut novel category," Kiran announced. We must be present during the Sunday ceremony.

Sheetal gave a congrats in return.

Though Kiran was expecting a more enthusiastic response, she wasn't taken aback.

"Why weren't you shocked?", inquired Kiran.

"Keerthan informed me about this early," Sheetal remarked with a giggle.

After a brief moment of euphoria fading, Kiran stated, "This fellow ruined the moment." Why didn't you inform me of this earlier, then?

Sheetal glared at him and said, "Well, I wanted to see the excitement in your shining eyes."

Kiran reddened.

A sizable crowd had gathered there on the day of the award ceremony.

Kiran, Sheetal, and his parents were also present. Kiran was clothed in a black and white suit, while Sheetal was dressed in a silver saree.

"Adv. Kiran Manohar is the winner of the best debut novel," the publisher declared.

The chief guest awarded the prize to Kiran as he came onto the stage.

The event's anchor introduced Kiran and welcomed him for speaking.

"Thank you, sir, for this award," Kiran remarked shortly after he took the mic. Above all, I express my gratitude to the public for their support. I value your support, dear readers.

A young man from the audience put up his hand.

"Do you have any questions?" Kiran inquired.

The young man said, "Yes sir, there is a rumour that the story of your book is based on your real life. So my question is where is your travel companion?"

With a smile, Kiran left the stage and approached Sheetal, inviting her to the stage and holding out his hand. She held his hand and went with him to the podium.

It said, "She is my fiance."

"Soon to be your life companion, right?" asked the audience with joy.

After exchanging quick looks, they both nodded.

It was she who recommended that I write stories, Kiran stated. In the end, I decided to turn our story into a book. We are grateful that you accepted our story.

The audience admired the pair.

Kiran's parents complimented each other on their son's choice.

Epilogue

On this day last year, by coincidence, they had crossed paths and ended up travelling together.

They would formally become life companions today.

Most people view a marriage ceremony as a chance to exhibit how much money you can spend on luxury. They often forget there is life after marriage, blowing a tonne of cash on a few days of celebration.

Kiran and Sheetal had decided to make prudent choices regarding their finances.

Our travel companions were sufficiently developed to understand the value of money. Their goal was not to showcase their financial status but to have a modest wedding.

Everyone in the auditorium was engaged.

Workers were setting up the seats and decorating the mandap and wedding hall.

The cantering team was hard at work preparing Sadhya, the Malayali wedding feast.

The bride's makeup was being done by Angelina's makeup crew.

The guests from the two families began to fill the wedding hall.

The ideal opportunity for people to reunite with friends and family is during the wedding festivities.

At last, Sheetal, our beautiful bride, was ready.

She was dressed in a traditional saree of peacock blue. The gold jewellery on display complemented her looks.

Sheetal's parents admired her gorgeous appearance, reflecting her serene and calm demeanour in her wedding look.

Her parents had admired the gorgeous appearance of Sheetal.

The bridegroom and his family arrived at the wedding venue.

In a traditional white shirt and white Mundu, a traditional dhoti with a golden border, Kiran looked handsome. He radiated refinement and elegance from the way he looked. He was adorned with a gold bracelet.

With customs, the bride's family embraced the groom's family.

They guided him into the hall and arranged for him to be seated in the mandap according to the customary rites.

It was magnificent to see the bride arrive in the customary manner and to the accompaniment of the customary rhythms.

Kiran gave her a meaningful gaze.

"She looks gorgeous in her saree. I love her.

Kiran got up from the Mandap as Sheetal came onto the stage.

The bride and groom sought their parents and elders for blessings.

Kiran entered on the stage and clasped his hands to greet the guests and seated on the mandap. Sheetal greeted the guests and sat in the Mandapa.

They exchanged glances and smiled. Their smile was significant in a lot of ways.

At the time of Muhurtham, the priest handed over the sacred thread to the groom after the customary ceremonies.

In the midst of flowers and the lively beats of traditional instruments, Kiran tied the sacred thread or Thali."

At last, they formally become life companions.

They later exchanged the lotus garlands.

Sheetal saw her elder sister standing close to the guests, clothed in a white churidar.

Her appearance appeared divine.

With a smile on her face and a sign of blessing, Thennal quietly faded.

Kiran gestured at what happened.

With a smile, Sheetal gave a gentle, horizontal head shake.

Despite knowing it was an illusion, she was delighted.

The customary rites were completed, marking the end of the fortunate occasion.

Guests had gone to indulge in the wedding feast, known as Sandya's.

Every wedding day must include a group of middle-aged women who enjoy chatting and reviewing information on the bride, groom, family, decoration, and—most importantly—the jewellery of the bride.

Unintentionally, Keerthan had taken his place in front of this team.

"The bride appears gorgeous, but I've heard that her family didn't give the groom's family enough money."

"Yes, I am familiar with this girl. She is an arrogant woman."·

"Oh, I see. I've heard that the groom paid for this wedding as well."

"That is just awful. How much pavan of gold is she wearing, then?"

"Let me say it," Keerthan said as he jumped into the conversation.

The gossip team momentarily became nervous.

Afterwards, a woman inquired to avoid awkwardness, saying, "Well, your wedding is next, son." When are we able to go to your wedding?

"Aunty, if you wish to attend my wedding, then I will marry your daughter," Keerthan retorted.

In response, the woman said, "Sorry, she is already engaged."

"I will never get a girl," Keerthan murmured to himself.

The groom and bride were busy while guests arrived to offer congratulations.

Kiran and Sheetal's co-workers, as well as their friends and family.

Nihal arrived at the wedding with his wife. Nihal and his wife attended their first event together as a married couple.

Olivia, Jacob, and Grace were invited as well. "Did you eat?" inquired Kiran.

"Yes, the feast was nice," Jacob replied. Kudos to the workers of the catering agency.

"My father-in-law arranged this," Kiran remarked.

Sheetal smiled.

"I never expected you to guys get married at last," Grace retorted.

It's a play of destiny, Kiran remarked with a smile.

Jacob stated, "This is my first time at a wedding in Kerala. Everything was modest and elegant."

"You guys look so beautiful in this attire," Grace said. Made for each other.

Sheetal and Kiran exchanged a quick smile.

"I appreciate your effort to attend our wedding after travelling this much," Sheetal remarked.

Grace replied, "You are my little sister, so there is no need for a second thought."

"All the best for your new beginning," was Jacob's response.

While the day of the wedding is a time for celebration, the bride and groom will also likely feel worn out from smiling for so many pictures.

The event is finally over.

After the customary practices, the groom and bride were required to go to the groom's home.

As the bride and groom entered the car, Keerthan took control of the car.

Keerthan inquired, "So, how will you guys stay in Kollam?" while on the road. Both of you work in Trivandrum.

"After the leave, we will move to Sheetal's house," Kiran declared. I don't care if our beloved relatives assume less of us. Since you are with my parents, Keerthan, I know you will look after them. Since Sheetal is their only daughter, we must look after them.

Sheetal softly held Kiran's hands.

"We don't want to consider the opinions of others," Keerthan retorted. I will take care of our parents, so don't worry, bro."

"Are you happy, Keerthan?" inquired Kiran.

In response, Keerthan remarked, "I'm overwhelmed about you guys, but my mother told me I'm not old enough to get married.

They chuckled.

"Keerthan, try to find a girl by yourself," Sheetal advised.

"Sis, I don't believe in love marriage," Keerthan remarked. I'll wed the woman my family selects.

There was a smile on both of their faces.

"Are you teasing me?" inquired Kiran.

"No, it's my opinion lol," Keerthan retorted.

"Then wait patiently, brother," Sheetal responded.

Keerthan gave a nod.

"Well, where is our honeymoon?" inquired Sheetal.

"We can't afford Malaysia and Singapore countries," Kiran retorted. I assume you are aware of the funds.

With a smirk, Sheetal replied, "No, I don't want to go there."

"Any place we had travelled before?" inquired Kiran.

Sheetal gave a nod.

Kiran enquired, "Mumbai?"

"My favourite place was Mumbai. I'm not sure. You move forward," Kiran remarked

"How about taking a sea voyage in Bangalore for our honeymoon?" Sheetal asked with a smile.

Kiran cried out, "No," feeling both frightened and anxious at the same moment.

They chuckled and hugged.

Keerthan pondered as he observed their image in the rearview mirror,

"I hope this happiness lasts forever for them."

"Kiran bro didn't search for a partner He was focused on his life and the people in it. Finally, he found a companion he deserved. I decided to focus more on my life, and I hope that she will eventually enter it. With a smile, Keerthan pondered, "I'm prepared to wait for her.

The authentic journey of Kiran and Sheetal as life companions began.

Kiran and Sheetal's journey was marked by constant talking, unending listening, disagreements, problem-solving, impatience, and composure.

Despite having distinct characteristics, their love and understanding strengthened and enriched their relationship.

"If life bores you?

If you want to take a break from a stressful life?
Pack your bags and go for a trip

But beware of the fund and safety.

Bon voyage"

About The Author

Keerthana Sarin is a young Indian author who began writing at the age of nine. She used to post poetry and short stories for her YouTube channel before publishing a psychological thriller debut novel, "Who is the Serial Killer?" Her second book, which is a different genre from her first one, reflects her experimentation with various literary genres.

You can connect with me on:-
https://www.instagram.com/keerthanasarin_author